The Long Dark

An Alaska Winter's Tale

*For Cynth,
Who knows there is more
in the wind than just the
music,*

Slim Randles
2005

The Long Dark

An Alaska Winter's Tale

by **Slim Randles**

McRoy & Blackburn, Publishers
Ester, Alaska

© 2002 by Slim Randles
revised edition

Published in Alaska by
McRoy & Blackburn, Publishers
P.O. Box 276
Ester, AK 99725
U.S.A.

mbe@mosquitonet.com
www.alaskafiction.com

All rights reserved.

Printed in the United States of America by
Thomson-Shore, Inc.
7300 West Joy Road
Dexter, MI 48130-9701

Book design and production by
Deirdre Alida Helfferich
Ester Designworks
P.O. Box 24
Ester, AK 99725

ISBN 0-9706712-1-0

printed on recycled, acid-free paper

to
Amanda Lois Randles Stossel
with love;
this look at your heritage

chapter 1

The loons watched that morning as the first fall flights of geese crossed their lake. The loons would soon follow.

The man walked down from the cabin to the lake, smashed some of the brittle shore ice with a stomp of his boot and filled his water buckets. Siwash Simmons smoked his pipe, looked at the loons and flared his nostrils against the cold bite of morning air. For more than forty years this man had been coming to stand on the shore of this lake; once again, he savored the sliver of time when the world was preparing to change.

The first ice clutched at the roots along the edge of the lake. The geese and ducks called as they flew for the warmer regions. The velvet sheaths were off the antlers of the moose and caribou bulls as they readied for war. The bears would be pacing the high tundra constantly now, gorging on the sweet bite of berries against the long sleep.

Simmons rubbed his beard, smiled and waved at the loons, sending them swimming toward the beaver lodge. He laughed and looked at the sky, his old gray eyes searching the scattered clouds for clues, for hints to the severity of the winter that was almost upon him, and looking for the plane bringing his dogs back to the cabin at the lake. The thick gray smoke of a new fire poured from the stovepipe as Simmons walked back up the trail. He looked with pride on the stack of firewood, thought about the arrival of his dogs, and made a mental note to comb his hair in honor of the occasion.

The loons saw the old man go into the cabin and heard the pleasant clink of the lids dancing on pots growing hot on the stove. They swam slowly back into shallow water and watched for minnows and sticklebacks.

From 2,000 feet, the taiga belt of forest slipped by beneath the plane, twinkling like a varicolored carpet. The gold and rust of fall were yielding to the starkness of barren birches and the charcoal green of the spruce. Buck Davis loved this time of year. Each season has its consolations, and the abrupt end of fall brought with it the savoring of final flights in the floatplane and the exciting prospects of the quick agility of a ski plane.

The dimpled gray of muskeg swamp slipped by, broken by an occasional moose trotting high-kneed away from a pond. Buck swung the wide floats more to the east, and gazed down at the lumpy silhouette of the plane skimming across forest that would have taken weeks to traverse on foot.

The mountain was hidden in clouds that day, except for the jagged glacier ends poking out the bottom. The clouds roughly covered the wild river valley, and the Cessna 185 began encountering them as it headed east. As each cloud approached the plane, Buck would involuntarily duck his head and grin at himself. The morning was a gem, cut sharply by the snap in the air, holding the country still and alert. Buck reached down and ruffled the ears of one of Siwash's dogs that had stuck his head between the front seats. All three were asleep. There hadn't been room for them in the plane that took Siwash to his cabin just a few weeks earlier.

"You boys comfortable?" he asked, then answered immediately, "Why certainly, Captain Davis. We especially enjoyed the meal and the dancing girls, and how about playing us a tune?"

"You gentlemen have any particular favorites?" he asked. The dogs looked up at him. Buck gave his best attempt at a bark and said, "Well, Captain, do you know 'Ride of the Valkyries' by Wagner?"

"Of course, fellas, but it's too nice a day for that. How about a taste of 'Jinny Git Around'?"

Buck pulled the harmonica out of his jacket pocket and began the sweet, bright music that was barely audible against the roar of the engine. The dogs perked up their ears and then went back to sleep. Buck's habit of talking to himself in the airplane was embarrassing only when he found the passengers looking strangely at him. Especially when he had forgotten he had passengers.

The loons looked up from their work at the sound of the engine and flew off. Siwash Simmons appeared in the door of his cabin, hastily combing his beard and smiling. The engine noise seemed a civilized symphony in the utter quiet of the forest, and would be enjoyed for its brief reminder of other places. The sound of the engine was nearly as welcome to Simmons as the disappearance of the sound would be later, when silence recaptured the forest.

As he swung into the downwind leg, sweeping low over the lake and the cabin, Buck Davis checked the ribbon tied to the stick near the lake, the simple device locally known as an "Alaska windsock." The ribbon confirmed Buck's appraisal of the wind direction and strength. He watched the great floats beneath him swing into the far turn. He throttled back gently, saw the lone spruce tree on a point of land disappear beneath him, and dropped the plane gently onto the lake. The dogs still slept.

Siwash waited at the end of the short dock and tied the floats to the rings. The men shook hands.

"Got some passengers for me, Buck?"

"Maybe. Got a crowbar?"

"Crowbar? What for?"

"Those dogs of yours like my plane so much they decided to spend the winter in it. Come on out, boys."

The dogs bounded out and jumped on Siwash, and the five walked up to the cabin.

"Time for some coffee, Buck?"

"I've always got time for coffee."

Buck recalled with a twinge of pain the first time he had flown to this cabin more than twenty years before, and was asked the same question. In the rush of youth, Buck had wanted to get back to the village and had told Simmons he was in a hurry, and would take a rain check.

"That's the trouble with young people," Simmons had said, looking hurt. "They're always in too much of a hurry to visit a spell."

Buck had found the time that day, and on every flight since. Only a full-blown emergency could keep him from having the coffee and the hospitality that was so important to these occasional hosts.

"Well, what's new in town?"

Siwash poured coffee and swept the huskies out the door with a broom. Buck looked around the cabin. The floor was swept, the magazines were stacked neatly, the dishes clean. Necessity and a small living space made Simmons, like most sourdoughs, an immaculate housekeeper.

Like a practiced town crier, Buck Davis gave the news as shortly and sweetly as he could.

"The Hunter family's mare had a colt. Yep, a little stud. Bay like the mother. Looks good. Frank Granger had another accident. Seems he got drunk and broke two ribs. Fell on a widow woman while dancing. Nope... just mashed her corsage, that's all. Coffee's six bucks a pound. Yeah, I know. Tea just don't have no substance, but we may have to get used to it. Tried that once, too, but spruce tea is still tea, and just doesn't make it. Hemingway Jones wrote a poem about it...the coffee, not spruce tea. Can't remember it, but you know how he is. It's full of Shakespeare-type words. We thought he had a girlfriend a while back, but she decided to stay with the tour and go back to Iowa. Yeah, smart."

"Sounds like civilization is managing to keep going OK without me, Buck."

"That's a matter of opinion. When you want to come out?"

"Don't know for sure. Check with me after freeze-up. I'll wait until a good snow to make my marten sets. If we get some decent snow this winter, we should have a good season."

"Siwash, what kind of a winter you figure?"

"Lots of snow. Cold, too, I imagine."

"Way I figure it, too."

"That boy of yours still flying the flame tails?"

"Yep. Sam thinks those jets are the only way to go, I guess."

"I always kinda figured he'd be flying with you by now."

Buck Davis stared into the coal black of his coffee. "Well, this kind of starve-to-death business isn't for everyone, I guess."

"Ain't nothin' finer than being a bush pilot, Buck, and you know it. Imagine trying to bring in a 737 on floats?"

"Man'd need the ocean, I guess."

Buck grinned at the thought. "Like to see one of those captains set a big one down on that gravel bar in the Tokositna River…"

"Yep!" The old man laughed. "You know, if that was my boy, I believe I'd have a word with him!"

"Sometimes words don't count for much, Siwash. It's darn hard to argue with that steady money."

"There's something to that, I suppose," Siwash said.

Buck did the honors on coffee. "What do you hear from over the ridge?"

"Was over there last week, and the mayor of Lynx Lake is looking poorly, Buck. Wish you'd look in on him."

"Figured to check on Kelly today."

"You know," Simmons said quietly, "old Pete has more imaginary diseases than forty old women, but I think something's really wrong with him this time."

"He's something, all right. The last time I was in there, he planned to leave his feet to science. Said something about grafting them onto a cheechako so the newcomer could run around the woods on really tough feet!"

"That man thinks he's a scientist, Buck. Honest. We was pardnered up along about twenty years ago for a few seasons, you know, and he like to drove me crazy with them scientific experiments. He thought for a while he could harness lightning bolts to cure insanity. Darn near burned the cabin down. When I yelled at him about it, he said the experiment failed, 'cause I was still crazy."

"Well, a man can get peculiar notions living all by himself at Lynx Lake."

"Peculiar? Well, I guess. Maybe he really ought to go in for a checkup, Buck."

"I'll drop in there today, and thanks for the coffee."

The dogs romped around Buck on the way out to the plane, but ran back when the engine started. The four residents watched the takeoff, waiting for the customary waggle of wings as the plane crossed the ridge and became an invisible hum in the background.

• • •

From Simmons Lake a trail climbed over a steep hogback ridge and meandered along a creek for several miles before coming to Lynx Lake. At the far end of the lake was a cabin, and unlike the interior of Simmons' place, this one was a rat's nest.

Stacks of magazines dating back years made moving from the single bunk to the stove treacherous. The magazines would have dated back further than that, but a fire fifteen years earlier had erased a twenty-year collection of scientific, medical and outdoor journals. It had also eliminated that cabin.

In stark contrast to the confusion of the present cabin, Pete Kelly always kept himself remarkably clean and well-dressed. He shaved daily and washed thoroughly, knowing for a certainty that dirt hid germs that would destroy a man's body before he knew what happened. His clean clothes, also, were the latest in backwoods fashions, according to the experts at L.L. Bean, Cabela's and Eddie Bauer.

Pete lay back on his bunk, holding in one hand the microphone of a battery-operated cassette recorder. He pushed buttons, then frowned as he flipped the microphone switch. He looked to be sure the reel was turning, then spoke deliberately into the mike.

"Now this tape is for Siwash Simmons living over at the next lake. This is Pete Kelly, and whoever finds my body, please see to it that my niece Sherry gets this place and the traps and all."

Pete switched off the microphone and played back what he had said. Smiling in satisfaction, he pushed the buttons again and continued.

"Now Si, I want you to see that this tape gets into the proper hands and all, and I know you will. The reason I'm doing this is, well, you know how everybody dies sometime, but nobody knows what dyin' is really all about. Nobody. Even those guys they give heart massage to...they may know...but they ain't tellin.' Now, I figger if a man's got a right to know anything in this life, it's what dyin' is all about...got me? I mean...everybody does it, don't matter what his beliefs is, or if he's a Communist or if he's a colored or if he's a Eskimo...he still dies."

Pete switched off the machine while he coughed. The coughing aggravated the pain in his chest and made him gasp for breath. When it stopped, he resumed.

"Sorry, Simmons, old pard...had to cough. Now where was I? Oh yes, the part about everybody dies. Well, Si, being as how I'm interested in medical stuff and such, I thought to myself, What can I leave behind to help people? This old body would more than likely get rejected if I gave it to somebody...'less they wanted it for bait, maybe. Well, I got to thinkin' that if a man had some warning of when he was going to die, you know, like these chest pains I'm havin', and this hard time breathin' and all. Well sir, he could make a tape recording of how it actually feels to die so others would know. You remember the story of that girl what almost drowned down in California there on the beach? They got her all pumped out later…but she said that while she was busy drowning she saw lots of pretty colors and heard beautiful music and all that. Now of course she didn't die. And that's the thing to remember, Si, she didn't die.

"She might have been just making up a story, or she might've seen those colors and all. Hell, lots of people almost die. So anyway, I gets this idea…that is, if I got this little tape machine, I can describe to people exactly what it's like to die, the real thing, you know, so's they'll know for sure. Chances are it won't be too bad. Maybe there will be pretty colors and organ music and such. I made a list of things to look for, but I guess we'll know pretty quick now.

"Now just picture what'll happen when this tape is revealed to the science world. Boy, that'll be something! Of course, I won't be here to see it, but it'll be something, I can tell you. You'll probably be a celebrity or something, you know, for bein' my partner and all. Glad to do it, Siwash.

"This'll sure be different from most people dyin', won't it? It'll be a damn sight better than Shorty when he got froze to death after going through the ice that time…you remember, Siwash? Ol' Shorty just layin' there sayin' I sure am cold'…course ol' Shorty never did know overflow ice from parboiled owl puke anyway. Well, I'll see you on the other side… s'long…"

Pete Kelly got out of bed and started slowly for the kitchen table where he'd left his makin's, but he didn't get there. He didn't hear Buck's plane buzz the cabin and land, either. The next thing he knew, it felt as if someone was jumping up and down on his chest. He opened his eyes and focused them on the worried-looking face of Buck Davis, who was pushing on his chest, over and over again.

Kelly lifted his hand up to his mouth, forgetting he didn't have the microphone with him, and said, "Siwash, the first thing you see when you're dead is Buck Davis."

Buck laughed.

"You're not dead, you old fool, but you will be if we don't get you to town pretty soon."

"I can't go now, Buck," Pete said in a hushed voice, "I haven't finished dying yet. It's all in the plan…"

Buck stopped the massage and looked at Kelly.

"You mean you want me to go away without you now, let you die, and then come back after you…"

"Yep. That's the plan."

Buck rubbed his forehead and thought a minute. "Now Pete, I'm here now and can take you in. Right?"

"Yeah."

"But if I wait until you're dead and then come back after you, that'll have to be charter rates. You got enough money for charter rates?"

"No. You'll have to trust me for it."

"I have a policy, Pete. Never trust a dead man."

And so Pete Kelly flew to town with Buck Davis, and lived.

chapter 2

WHEN THE South Seas Roadhouse was built, it was just the Roadhouse. As the years went by and the nearby mining area flourished, another roadhouse was built down the mud street and named the Kahiltna Roadhouse. Not to be outdone, the Roadhouse's owner, Frank Granger, named his business the South Seas Roadhouse. This choice was made partly because the local artist could paint nothing but palm trees for the shaping of the sign.

As the mines waned, so did the population of Kahiltna, until there was only enough business for one roadhouse. The die-hard settlers in the village divided their time and money equally between the two and waited to see what happened. Finally, one cold night in December, the Kahiltna Roadhouse solved the problem by burning down.

After fifty years of abusive weather, the sign read "S ut Se s Roadh u e," and the palm trees had been erased, trunks first, until only some fronds were left at the top. Tourists often mistook them to be fiddlehead ferns.

In a small Alaska village, the roadhouse is more than rooms, food and drink. Within its walls marriages are made and lost, as is an occasional fortune. Despite state laws to the contrary, dogs and children are welcomed there. The children are forbidden to drink. Many of the dogs are too. People died there, gave birth there, formulated plans to get rich there, went broke there, laughed there, cried there…and drank there.

During the Depression, an attempt was made to turn a profit in the South Seas Roadhouse. The experiment lasted two weeks, and consisted of an import from Anchorage—a woman named Ruby. It was a great party, but the owner counted a net loss on the deal of more than $30 due to the cost of medication for twenty-seven men and one woman.

The floors had long since been worn smooth and the doors didn't fit properly. The rooms upstairs were cold in winter, and middle C on the piano had been dead for thirty years. Some said Wild Bill had purloined the C string to repair a snowshoe, but no one was ever able to prove it.

The structure was insulated with six inches of sawdust, and would have been condemned by the volunteer fire department but for two things: the volunteers had no other place to hold their meetings, and there was no record of the building's existence. On paper down in the green borough building in Palmer, at any rate, it didn't exist. The village site was laid out years after the buildings in it had been built, so cabins sometimes straddled two lots and half of a street. Extrapolating from the official plat on which it didn't exist, the South Seas Roadhouse occupied half of one street and a portion of the village square. A building must exist to be condemned. It must also exist to be owned or taxed. Frank Granger was the only man who claimed to have seen the building built. The others had all died years before, and no one could dispute his ownership.

There were several men in the village who had lived there nearly as long as Frank. Their credit was always good for a beer at the South Seas, and whenever they were asked who owned the roadhouse, they always said, "Frank."

Beneath the wolf pelt on the far wall was a bulletin board, and the residents of the Kahiltna area checked the board for interesting items or messages as unconsciously as a teenager checks the icebox when he isn't hungry.

Antlers, photos and smoke stains were the wall decorations, and laughter the rule. The South Seas was the hub and soul of Kahiltna. The coming of several churches did not change this. The South Seas Roadhouse was a place where an old gold miner could dance with a tiny infant, and dogs slept next to the oil heater in accordance with an elaborate pecking order.

The Health Department inspector once threatened to close down the business if the dogs weren't removed. Frank tried to jump over the bar with a pool cue, but was restrained. Finally he just looked at the inspector and said, "Them are healthy dogs, every one. Dogs are fellas same as anyone, and need to sleep by the stove. Besides, you can't shut down a business that doesn't exist. Look it up."

Nothing more was ever said about the dogs.

Tourist-baiting was the favorite South Seas pastime each summer, but the cold air of autumn had driven most of them to warmer climes so only a solitary tourist lady was listening to John Thompson tell how many times he'd been killed by bears.

Frank Granger was making a young couple—Melody and Dave, they said—welcome at one of the tables, and at the next table sat Buck Davis and his son, Sam. Harry Pete, whose ancestors had lived in Kahiltna since long before it was a part of the United States, was talking to the bartender, Hemingway Jones, over coffee.

"Did you read that first chapter of my novel, Harry?"

The Indian nodded and smiled.

"Well?"

"Well what?"

"What did you think of it?"

Harry Pete stared at his coffee. His mouth worked studiously and solemnly. Finally he said, "Isn't that the same chapter you showed me last year, Hemingway?"

"Well, I rewrote it last spring."

"It's very…exciting."

"You really think so?"

"Yes."

"In what way?"

"Well, ten murders in the first chapter is exciting, Hem."

The bartender brightened.

"That's how I figured it, too. You have to catch the reader's attention right away. Fame is so fleeting, alas…"

"But what I'd like to know is, who killed all those people, Hemingway? I mean, at the rate you're writing this, I may not live long enough to read the whole thing."

"That's the problem."

"Problem?"

"Yeah. I don't know yet who did it."

The saddened face of the bartender stifled any remark from Harry.

Sam Davis was a younger version of Buck, but with darker hair and eyes. His mother always credited her son's dark good looks to her grandfather, who had lived in Kahiltna since before white men came to the village. His name had been unpronounceable to them, and so the early miners had called him Pete. Harry Pete was also his grandson.

After the men had exchanged the news, Buck asked, "How long you home for?"

"Just a few days, dad. I'll be starting the Anchorage to Fairbanks run soon."

"Which flight?"

"Eight forty-six. I'll think about you when I go over the village."

Buck grinned.

"You mean you'll be thinking about those stews in the back."

"They're flight attendants now," Sam said with a grin, "and some of them are guys. Though I admit one or two of the ladies…Well," he pulled on his ear and screwed up his mouth in a bad imitation of his father's habit, "I'll be thinking how nice it would be to have one of those stews down here at the South Seas."

"OK, I can believe that."

Buck slowly sipped his beer.

"You know," he said, "old Siwash thinks you ought to give up the jets and fly with me."

"No thanks, dad," Sam smiled. "I like earning regular money."

"Of course," Buck said carefully, "you have to fly when they tell you and where they tell you to earn that money."

"But it's there, all the same, every payday."

"But, son, doesn't it bother you to wear a necktie and a uniform?"

Sam's dark eyes chuckled.

"I don't know, some of the women I know seem to like uniforms."

Frank Granger stood up and pronounced to the world, "Never, but NEVER, trust a woman who likes uniforms, Sam. It's a fact. If they like one uniform, they like them all. First thing you know, you've got competition from traffic cops, parking lot attendants, the mailman, and even the Alaska Air National Guard!"

"You tell him, Frank!" yelled Hemingway.

Sam and Buck joined the laughter that followed Frank's pronouncement. John Thompson said to the tourist lady, "There we hear from an expert on women of all types, ma'am."

"John," Frank growled, "I believe I'll cut off your credit."

"Now, Frank, aren't you the one who's writing to all the lonely ladies in Iowa? You see, ma'am…Frank…"

"Dammit, John, I am not! Oh, I might send a card or something once in a while, but…"

"Now, Frank," Buck said, "you mean to say all those ladies in that lonely hearts club aren't hearing regularly from their rugged sourdough with a heart big as the mountains?"

"Buck! I swear, someday I'll learn who it was put my name in for that lonely hearts club, and when I find out, there'll be hell to pay!"

"But Frank," John Thompson teased, "did you have to write to them all?"

The South Seas occupants roared as one, as Frank's antics through the mail were as well known as everything else that happened in the village.

Buck waved at Hemingway for two more beers, and the bartender put the beers down on the table with a flourish.

"In thy vats our cares be drowned, with thy grapes our hairs be crowned!"

"What'd he say, Sam?"

Hemingway scowled. "It's Shakespeare's tribute to wine."

"I'll stick with Oly," Buck grinned.

Sam looked steadily at his father. 'What makes you keep going, dad? Flying out here, I mean. You could've done a lot of other things and made more money."

"You mean working for somebody else?"

"That's it, then?"

Buck nodded. "Part of it, anyway. The rest has to do with flying."

"Don't you wish you had someone else do all that mechanic work, though?"

"On the majors, I do have someone else do it. But on the little stuff, I'd rather do it myself. You know how many pilots have never been seen again up here because some mechanic's nineteen-year-old apprentice forgot to tighten a nut? Neither do I, and we never will. That's why I do it myself."

"But bush flying doesn't pay that well."

"Can you park that 737 and go ice fishing when you feel like it?"

"No. Can you look down on the mountain from 35,000 feet?"

"No. Can you stop in for coffee at Siwash's cabin?"

Sam grinned.

"My coffee is delivered. And the deliverer is much better looking than Siwash Simmons, which makes it a lot nicer for the deliveree, which is me." They laughed, but there was a hint of hurt on Buck's face. Melody got up from the table and excused herself to Frank Granger and her husband. The two men watched her go upstairs. "Nice lady you got there, son," said Frank.

"Thanks, Frank. I know she'll like it out there," Dave said.

"How about you?"

"I've dreamed about doing this all my life. I've never trapped, but I'm going to do my best. We'll make out OK, I think."

"Ever made a set for marten?"

"Not yet."

The tall old man shaped his hands together like a tent. "Make a little lean-to like this out of sticks. Drives 'em nuts, you know. Those marten think they're the smartest things in the woods, and they just gotta figure out what it is. Put one set inside the little lean-to and two more out from it a ways. Might pick up a mink that way, too."

"You trap a lot, Frank?"

"Did some years ago. Been here in the South Seas most of the time. Picked up a lot of information from experts over the years, though. Trouble is figuring which to believe and which to laugh at."

"I hope I can make enough this winter to last us." Dave looked down at his strong hands.

"You know, kid," Frank said with a toss of his head toward the stairs, "you have a woman to look after now. The most important thing to remember is that women are funny about the Bush. Never seen a woman yet who felt comfortable about living in the Bush. Enthusiastic sometimes. Terrified occasionally. But never comfortable. There's two kinds of women in Alaska, boy. There's the kind that take one look and want to be on the first plane south. We don't have to worry about them. Then there's the other kind that you couldn't pry out of the boonies with a crowbar. Those are the ones we have to deal with. They are never truly comfortable. They will sit there and tell you straight-faced that they came to the boonies to escape civilization. They are tired of the hustle and bustle of the city. They want peace and quiet and freedom. That lasts about a month." Frank raised a hand. "Now don't get me wrong. They are wonderful ladies, and life wouldn't be much fun without 'em, God bless 'em each and every one. It's just you have to understand how things are, Dave.

"Now when they go out to these cabins, they think it's an adventure going to the outhouse. They love the feeling of freedom when they go down to the creek to haul water. They feel biblical when they trim the wicks on the kerosene lamps. Then they read a story on how you need so many candlepower of light to keep from going blind while reading. That leads to a nasty hissing Coleman lantern, which any fool can tell you is just an eye blink away from having to have your own generator in a shed out back and electric light bulbs. No, now let me finish. So when the creek freezes over and the ice has to be chopped through at forty below to get water, the idea of a hand pump in the cabin sure looks attractive. So you dig a well and put in the pump. By this time, you've got that generator humming away and burning diesel half the time anyway, so why not just hook up a submersible pump and install a holding tank and save all that hand pumping. Right?

"Well, to keep that tank of water from freezing solid overnight when the fire is down, you'll have to put in an oil heater. And now that the cabin is warm all the time, and the water is being pumped, it's just natural that it would be nice to have an indoor privy, which means digging a hole in the yard for a septic tank."

Frank took a long pull at his beer.

"Well, kid, the only problem with having a septic tank is that you can't fly it in, so you clear a good wide trail for it through the woods, and sled it in during the winter from the nearest road. By this time, the money you are spending to have Buck fly in all that diesel and heating fuel and replacement light bulbs is enough to bankrupt the city of Winslow, Arizona. So you get to looking at that nice wide trail you cut through the woods, and you get to thinking how handy it would be to be able to drive a truck back in to your cabin there. Of course, renting the equipment it would take to do that takes more money than a man can make trapping, so you'll have to leave and get a job. If you work steady, you'll be flying back and forth a lot until the road is built, which will cost more money. So you have to take a weekend job to pay for the flights that you don't have time to take any more."

Dave was looking stunned.

"Now don't get me wrong, son. It's not all that bleak. See, before long you'll have that road built, and be able to drive back and forth to work. Of course, it'll take two hours of driving each way, which cuts down on your time at the cabin, and the little lady will begin to worry about the safety of the babies."

"Babies?"

"Why hell, yes, babies! Why, don't you know how Mama Nature works up here in the Bush? Just as soon as that generator starts to hum and the submersible pump allows a woman to stay indoors for a while, all those mysterious little woman-type things begin to happen, and they start to get these little funny Mona Lisa smiles at odd hours, and the first thing you know you're a daddy.

"Well, as I was saying, they get to worrying about stuff like 'What would I do if the baby drinks three gallons of diesel and Dave isn't here?' So the next project is getting a telephone. For Emergencies Only. It's always For Emergencies Only. Well sir, by the time the phone company has strung twelve miles of cable and poles through the muskeg swamp, you're in debt for the next thirty-four years."

Dave was ashen-faced.

"Now Davie-boy, I don't want you to get discouraged, because you'll just be fitting into the Alaska Way of Life. It's the Alaska thing to do to escape civilization, go as far back in the boonies as you can, and then figure how to take the television and electric toaster with you."

"That doesn't sound very encouraging, Frank."

"Well," Frank glanced nonchalantly out the window, "there's only one way to prevent all that from happening, son."

A glimmer of hope appeared on Dave's face.

"How do I do that?"

"Well, if you'll recall, this whole problem began when she read a story about the candlepower of kerosene lamps, right?"

"Yes?"

"Well, then," Frank grinned and leaned across the table conspiratorially, "don't let her read!"

Frank turned and raised his glass to Melody as she reentered the barroom.

"Here's to the ladies. May God bless 'em each and every one!"

Melody smiled shyly, and Dave looked closely for any resemblance to Mona Lisa.

"It's snowing."

The softness of the words from Melody caused all heads to turn toward the windows. The first few flakes of winter came down and shrank and disappeared as they touched. There was a silence in the bar to match the ponderous silence outside. There is something magical, almost sacred, about the first snowfall in snow country. Everyone is left with his own thoughts and memories and expectations.

The only sound was the ballpoint scratching of Hemingway on his legal pad. Then that stopped.

"I wrote a poem about the snow," he said shyly.

"Well, let's hear it," said Buck.

"OK. Here's how it goes. Fluffy flakes of silence cover the ground
And the only sound is the heartbeat of the sleeping snowmachines…"

The bar patrons looked at one another, then nodded approval at Hemingway, who beamed and bought a round for the house.

"Our people have a little saying about the snow," Harry Pete said quietly. "I guess it's a poem that doesn't rhyme."

"Those are the best kind," said Hemingway knowingly.

"I'd like to hear it," said Melody.

"Yeah," Sam nodded with a smile, "fling it on us, Cousin Harry."

"Well," Harry Pete looked up for a minute and thought. "You want it in Athabascan or English?"

They laughed.

"OK, English then, but no promises on the translation."

The room went dead quiet.

"My grandmother used to tell it. Let's see. 'The Mother sees our cold, and…wraps us tightly for the long sleep…tucks us in until the sun pulls back our robes.'"

"That's beautiful," Hemingway whispered.

No one else spoke, but just watched the snow fall quietly, each with his own thoughts.

chapter 3

THERE IS A LIFE and a mystery to the first snowfall. The ground, heated by five months of sun, quickly melts the first flakes, moistening the ground. If the storm is serious, it can wait until the ground finally cools and begins to accept the inevitability of winter.

Old-timers of all races watch the first snow and check thermometers, adding all the factors to arrive at the annual prediction of what kind of winter it will be. Right or wrong, no one seems to notice, but all put much value on the conflicting reports the sages issue.

This time it snowed for three days. The snow began to stick after several hours, and the flakes came down in large clumps, obscuring the vista and closing the residents of Kahiltna snugly in their homes. They walked around their yards, picking up axes and shovels and ropes before they were buried. Farsighted individuals covered the woodpiles with plastic. Roofs slowly turned white, and then lay deep with the snow. Trails were packed to the post office, log library, trading post and the South Seas.

Early on the second morning, Kahiltna's pilots brushed the snow off the wings and looked for breaks in the clouds. There were none. On the third day, the floatplanes were hauled out of the encroaching ice, jacked up and the floats replaced with skis. Again the pilots looked in vain for a break in the weather.

Around the village, the snow crept into tiny crevices, icing over the roughness of stumps, fence posts, pickup trucks and trees. Spread smoothly and evenly, the snow changed the village during the three-day storm from a sharply angled group of rough brown objects to a warmly rounded ballet in white.

The storm stopped near midnight on the third day. By morning the insulating cloud layer had gone, and a pervading cold sank down on the village. Half the elementary schoolchildren stayed home with colds. The sled dogs whined with the weather's sting. Villagers had to relearn the identities of their neighbors for another season by parka design. Each parka hood exuded a cloud of steam when people walked.

Buck Davis and the other pilots walked to the local lake each afternoon, testing and prodding the ice with long chisels. They tested around the edges where the warm springs were, and nodded with knowing authority at the thickness of the ice. For days nothing flew.

Then the ice was tested again, there were knowing nods, and each plane roared off the ice into service to the far lakes. The Super Cubs and Arctic Terns were used first. If the ice held, the 170s and 185s would follow.

With practiced skill, Buck Davis flew alone to the remote lake where Dave and Melody were to live. He opened the window of the Cub as he dropped down to the lake, and wrestled a head-sized rock out of the window. It fell from a delicately predetermined height to the center of the lake ice, bounced twice, and skidded for about 100 feet. The lake passed Buck's first test. On the second pass, Buck set the Cub down close to the ice while maintaining good airspeed. In a series of rapid movements, he beat the skis on the frozen surface as he skimmed the lake, then pulled steeply up over the ridge on the far side and watched the ice. He circled twice, but saw no telltale overflow water on the lake. He landed the Cub lightly, then tested the ice with a chisel for depth. Satisfied, he walked to the cabin on snowshoes, built a fire in the heater, then flew back to town for the 185 and his passengers.

It was on the second haul to the cabin that it happened. Dave and Melody had been flown in without incident. The second haul consisted of groceries and other supplies, a chain saw and Dave's dog, Queenie. Queenie was a large white husky, exuberant in the friendliness that typifies the breed. She was stuffed into the rear of the big Cessna and lay with her head pointing forward between the front seats, comfortable on two sacks of dog food. It was getting close to dark now, in the premature twilight of midafternoon. The sun had gone from the white country below, and only the reflective powers of the snow made visibility possible. There would be no more flights today. Flying at 2,000 feet, Buck encountered a pocket of rough air. The bouncing airplane ruffled some ancient nerve of stability in the dog and she whined, then stood and tried to climb into Buck's lap. As Buck tried to shove her back she became frantic and hit the wheel, tilting the airplane violently. In the melee that followed, and despite everything Buck tried, Queenie's hind foot shoved the door handle and she went out of the plane. Banking quickly, Buck watched helplessly as the white dog fell, at first thrashing against the resisting air, then planing as she thrust all four feet out against the wind. She fell toward a frozen pond, as hard as concrete in the cold. But the vagaries of nature took a hand during the free fall. In the outspread position of a skydiver, Queenie began to track across the sky as she fell. Instead of meeting the crushing ice, she sailed across the pond and landed in deep drifts blown over the top of alder thickets at the pond's edge. In an explosion of snow, the dog hurtled into the covered brush, bounced high into the air, and then landed more gently. Buck jerked the flaps on the big plane and dropped lower and lower toward the crash site. Cruising just above the snow, he saw unexpected movement and then Queenie blew snow from her nose and staggered onto the ice of the pond, shaken but alive. Buck watched unbelievingly as the dog walked step by step on the pond, glancing up at the anxious passes of the plane. He circled the pond, then circled in ever-widening arcs as he searched for a landing spot. A mile away he found what he was looking for, a long, straight stretch of muskeg swamp with an even snow cover. He knew he could land the 185 on it, but he also knew for certain he would never be able to take off again with the larger plane. It would be no problem for the little Cub, but the darkness was coming down quickly, and the rescue flight would have to wait for first light. With a final look at the dog, Buck unconsciously wagged his wings at her in futile reassurance and flew back to the village.

There wasn't much sleep for Buck that night. He was silent through dinner, and Mary was careful not to interrupt his thoughts. The warmth of the house seemed to emphasize the contrast between Buck's place and the hollow in the snow that must be Queenie's abode for the night. The cold wouldn't bother Queenie, for she was a husky and knew how to handle it. She slept outside all year. But huskies are gregarious animals, as are their wild cousins, the wolves. And there is a fear lying deep within each of Alaska's sled dogs that is almost undetectable to all but the few who spend their lives with them. They fear solitude and the wolf. The far-off howl of the wolf sends all huskies burrowing deeper into the snow, where they lie still and quiet. The wolf is their enemy. Despite a common ancestry, the wolf cannot abide a dog and will kill and eat any he finds. And husky pups know this. The first time they hear that great diesel bawl from the yellow-eyed carrier of death they whimper and crawl closer together, and want to disappear into the earth.

At first light the Super Cub lifted from the village strip with a pair of trail snowshoes strapped to the struts. After an hour's flight Buck landed the Cub in a thin flourish of snow spray and bounced to a stop. He put on the shoes and slogged foot after foot to the frozen pond.

Buck followed the tracks to a snow-covered spruce and heard the soft growling before he saw Queenie. He spoke to her and tossed in a piece of dry fish. She awkwardly but enthusiastically ate the fish and staggered out to meet the pilot.

Buck hugged her gently and felt for broken bones. She was sore but intact, and the tears of relief froze on his face. He picked up the heavy dog as though she were a sheep and shuffled back along his snowshoe trail to the aircraft.

chapter 4

"You mean she got right back in the plane?"

Buck looked up at Frank Granger, smiled and shook his head in disbelief.

"Right back in, no hesitation. I couldn't believe it, either. So I flew her in to Dave and Melody's place, and she rode there like a dream. I wasn't taking any chances this time, though. I tied her up in the back."

"I hope to shout you would," said Frank.

Harry Pete looked over from his cup of coffee.

"You see, Buck, it's like I told you," he said. "Some folks will do just about anything to keep from flying with you!"

"I'll have to admit that's the first passenger I've had leave the airplane before I've asked them to, but Queenie more than made up for that."

"What do you mean?" said Frank.

"Well, I landed at Dave and Melody's place, and they ran out and hugged the dog and everything, but Queenie just wouldn't come out of the plane. It finally took all three of us to pry her out of there. She had wedged herself back in a corner and was braced for invasion. I guess she remembered the first time she got out of a plane and wasn't about to try it again!"

John Thompson drank his beer as the men laughed, then said, "That's what happens when a man has dogs. They're always doing something like that."

"When's the last time you heard of a dog jumping out of an airplane, John?" asked Harry.

"Well, I mean things like that, unexpected things. Now you take a snowmachine…"

"No. YOU take a snowmachine. I'll stick to dogs, thanks."

"That's the trouble with Indians these days," John laughed. "You raise 'em up, send 'em to college, and they go straight back to the village and say 'Me want run dog team. Go trap."

Harry Pete laughed with the rest of them, then narrowed his eyes and asked, "You saying a snowmachine can outdo a dog team, old-timer?"

"Any day of the week. And you don't have to feed it all summer."

"But what happens when it breaks down?"

"You fix it. What happens when you run out of dog food?"

"They eat the musher, of course," Harry said.

"Of course. Well, you have a dog team that can do sixty miles an hour?

"No."

"I've got a snowmachine that can."

"Not cross-country it can't. Not cross-country when there's no trail, and trees you have to go through. No, sir."

"Maybe not sixty. But plenty fast enough to leave your team of fish-burners behind." The men glared at each other with smiles curling their mouths.

Frank Granger took the floor. "Now, gentlemen, it appears that what we have here is a difference of opinion. Whenever there is a difference of opinion of this type, it is only fair and right to have a contest to see which is correct."

"A race!"

"Let's have a race!" the bar patrons yelled.

"I do believe that is in order," Frank said solemnly. Then, holding his hands out benevolently, he said, "If there be anyone present who knows why these two idiots should not engage in mortal race combat, let him speak now or forever…"

"I can't right now," Harry Pete said mournfully.

"Aha! I knew it!" John lifted his beer in a winning salute.

"Why not?" asked Frank.

"My dogs don't have any miles on them. I need a couple of weeks to toughen up Crabmeat and the boys."

"OK with you, John?"

"The more miles he puts on those pooches, the more tired they'll be. I'll be ready when he is."

"Then it's agreed," said Frank, smiling. "At the proper time, and at a place to be announced, a race will occur that will settle for all time the controversy between dogs and snowmachines. The best the eastern factories can turn out will go against Crabmeat, Kahiltna's own one-eyed wonder dog, and his faithful friends, of course. The race will be known as the World Championship Race to End All Controversy Between Dogs and Snowmachines, and will be duly recorded in local song and legend. Gentlemen," Frank gulped, "the drinks are on the house!"

A shout went up that could be heard at the trading post across the street, causing old Minnie Hunter to open the front door and see whether the village had burned down. She heard the laughter, smiled and walked back in to put up the canned pears.

chapter 5

MINNIE HUNTER'S HOME had soft, filmy curtains against the logs. The house was small but fine, sitting hidden behind the trading post. She had lived there for many years, and the nights and the living and the rare old-fashioned beauty of the occupant had worn and polished the house so it now resembled the owner.

A small house, with enough years, becomes like the shell of a tortoise; the house fits the person. Eccentricities showed in little ways. Alcoves of the house become repositories for alcoves of the mind, and Minnie Hunter's house fitted Minnie.

There was great care here, as though through polish she could maintain girlhood dreams from long ago. Keep the memories alive. And there were memories.

They were all so long ago now. The bloom of youth had faded with the dark hair Minnie once had treasured. Some memories also had faded, but others had ripened like fine wine. She remembered the old house on the sound where she had spent summers as a girl. But the memories now took so much effort. It had been so long. They were now sweeter and better. She remembered the dark staircase, and the large room upstairs she had shared with her sister. Now her sister was gone from this world, and gone from a different world from Minnie's. Her sister had chosen the cotillion and crocheting. Minnie had chosen a Dutch oven and snowshoes.

She smiled at the memories as she watched the fire slowly change in her tiny grate.

She was now getting old, and she could afford to be selective with her memories. Minnie preferred to remember the good things now; it was so much easier. The hard things, the bitter things, the disappointing barbs in a person's childhood—the instinctive lessons alone remained now. The hard memories had found their own dusty drawer years back.

The years in Kahiltna had drawn layer after layer of gauzy curtains over the early memories, each one so slight it was not noticed. One day, in attempting to look back to those more gracious years, she found the layers of curtains had blocked a clear view, leaving only the soft-focus warmth of smiles and love glowing through to reach the mind. How strange an effect this new land had on her.

It was a new land. It was new to her when she arrived as a young bride more than forty years ago, and it had not stopped being new. It had never attained the gentility of generations, as had her early home, but it had also never been accursed with the hint of dry rot and boredom. She still would willingly exchange the gentility and refinement for the verve and dash of life in this tiny village.

On evenings like this, when the thermometer dropped to dangerous levels and froze the world to a hushed reverence; when the rime climbed the windows; when the soft music of Vivaldi untangled the strictures of the day; then the memories came, and they were different. These last few seasons, the memories that came into focus were sweet remembrances of sitting high in a blueberry patch as the sun lit the tundra into a flame of blood-red leaves, watching the lordly strut of a rutting moose. Of laughing with the wonderful man, oh, so long ago now, who pulled her out of that snowbank and brushed away the flakes from her eyebrows and kissed her as he helped her back into the sled. Of a wedding, a painful, joyful, wonderful moment in the street in front of the trading post.

But there's no time for the memories now. Minnie replaced Vivaldi on the record player with the dancing fire of Smetana, and the stirrings of mischief began in her mind. This was Kahiltna. This was now, and the sweet playthings of the past would have to wait for another night.

She smiled at the flash of the music, and her young eyes sparkled with secret wanderings as she began to write.

It was a long letter, and in the firelight her eyes showed the duality of mischief and tenderness during the writing. She folded the letter and sealed it in an envelope, then put it in a larger envelope and sealed and addressed that one also.

She poured herself coffee as a treat and as a subliminal supplication to Pan, then smiled at herself as she looked at the larger envelope once more.

The knock on the door brought her back from her reveries, and she opened it quickly and handed the broom to Hemingway, who brushed the snow off his mukluks and closed the door.

"Saw your lights, Minnie, and wondered if you felt like some conversation."

"You know, Leon, I was just thinking how nice it would be to have a visit here by the fire. I have some coffee hot if you'd like some."

"Thanks. Love it. It's a cold one tonight. Heard it's supposed to stay like this for a few days."

"I like to think of it as paying our dues for the nice weather, Leon. But even with the cold, there are northern lights and lots of stars. Makes me feel like a young girl again. You take sugar?"

"Yes. Two, please. You know, Minnie, you're the only person in the village who calls me by my given name."

"Would you prefer I call you Hemingway like the others?"

"No. No, I really wouldn't. Hemingway isn't a bad name, I mean. I know they're mostly teasing by calling me that, but also, well, I like to think they mean it as a compliment, too. Because I want to write."

"I'm sure they do."

"You know, your calling me Leon makes me feel a little like I'm going home when I see you. It's a nice feeling. Like visiting the cookie jar again at my mother's house."

Minnie drew herself up straight and pretended to stare sternly at her guest.

"Young man, I may admit to having a few years on you, but your mother! Really!"

"I'm sorry, Minnie, I didn't mean…."

Her laughter changed the anguish in his face to a broad grin and he shook his head at her slowly.

"Honestly, I never know when you're for real or when you're joking."

"Good! Now tell me, how's your book coming?"

"Not good, I'm afraid. I don't think I have what it takes to be a writer. You know, writers have the 'divine discontent' that drives them on. Writing, you see, is one percent inspiration and ninety-nine percent perspiration. I guess all I can give it is ninety-nine percent."

"Mr. Jones, sir, it sounds very much to me like you've been reading too many books on writing. Reading about other people who are successful, in any field, can discourage a person, you know. I've read something about writing myself, over the years, and the one thing that sticks in my mind is that no one can teach another person to write. Only by actually writing can you learn. Had you heard that before, Leon?"

"Yes, I've heard that too."

Hemingway Jones leaned back and stretched against the lace doilies on Minnie's couch, then leaned forward, elbows on knees, and stared into the fire.

"It's just that I sit down to write and nothing happens. Well. A little, maybe. I'll get an idea, or actually a part of an idea, and I'll sit down and type it out, but then I can never think of what comes next."

Minnie leaned across and patted his hand.

"May I ask you something, as a friend?"

"Sure."

"What are you writing about? Some detective story, isn't it?"

"Yes, sort of a murder mystery."

"Why don't you write about something you know? Write about the things you understand, and about the people around you. It seems to me it would be a lot easier to write about life here in Alaska, and the people here in Kahiltna, than about life in a city where you've never lived."

"You may be right. No, I really think you're right. I can write about the snow and the cold nights like this one, and the practical jokes the fellas play on each other…and…"

"That's the spirit! It may not make a writer out of you immediately, of course."

"Of course."

"But it's bound to be a start, right?"

"Right." Hemingway stood and pulled on his parka. "I can't thank you enough, Minnie. I don't know if I can do it, but I'm going to try. You know, maybe I just can do it, too."

"Of course you can! Say, would you mind dropping this in the mail slot for me when you pass the post office, Leon?"

He took the envelope and said good night, then was swallowed up by the dark and the sting of the cold, totally unaware of the part he was playing in a future legend.

"His mother indeed!"

Minnie laughed, and looked around the cabin at the memories and then looked inside herself for a secret—and found one. She slept better that night than she had in ages.

chapter 6

THE MAN sitting beside Buck in the 185 was Cruchot. Hunter and Morris sat wedged in the back with the climbing gear. Buck looked over at Andre Cruchot and saw the stern look of defiance on the man's face as he stared straight ahead at the approaching mountain.

How cool these professionals are, he thought. The mountain is hard to climb in the summer, when the weather is comparatively mild. It is very hard to climb in the spring, when the avalanches are at their lowest ebb. But winter!

The white of the valley below became more pronounced as the land gradually rose, forcing the thinning spruce forest to recede even more. Ahead were rocks and ice. Vertical rocks.

In the South Seas the previous night, the mountain climbers had been the butt of the jokes.

"Buck," said John Thompson, "you know why those mountain climbers tie themselves together with ropes?"

"I have a feeling you're going to tell me."

"It's to keep the smart ones from going home!"

But through the laughter there was an unspoken respect for the men who were attempting the winter climb. For these mountaineers were men, like them, and men were getting harder to find these days. These men in nylon-covered parkas and steel crampons and aluminum pitons were the new crop of that breed who dared do things differently, and with little or no thought of personal gain. Beneath the surface these men were of a kind: The kind who panned for gold in Cache Creek fifty years before. The kind who came over the Chilkoot in '95. The kind who drove the dog teams to Nome each year in the Iditarod Race. The kind who flew the tiny airplanes in the winds of the mountain.

As the aircraft started over the toe of the serrated glacier, Cruchot looked up toward the peak. His eye traced the projected route up the Comb, as though from this distance of thirty miles he could spot some loose rock, some tiny crevasse, some ice cornice that could trip them up and wipe them out.

Cruchot thought only of the Alps and of his father. And of his father's death on the Eiger so many years before.

Hunter looked eagerly toward the mountain, unconsciously flexing his muscles as though he were walking up the rough white and aquamarine surface of the glacier rather than flying along its length to the airstrip at 7,200 feet. It was a chance to climb with Cruchot. It was a chance at the mountain. It meant repeating one semester in college. It was worth it.

Morris snapped one picture after another with his Leica, a present from the men at the office. It was an expensive gift, but then he owned the office. And the building. And two subsidiaries. After Cruchot had called, Morris began going to the health spa again. He still had about fifteen pounds to lose, but he would drop that on the mountain. Cruchot had to take him along. Morris had the money.

Buck's plane fought a headwind as the tiny craft climbed up along the rough tongue of the glacier. Then they were into the gorge, and the stark rock faces of the cliffs halted the men's thoughts.

When the gorge opened out, the men could barely make out the single pair of ski tracks Buck had made on the previous dunnage haul. They sighted the black speck that was their pile of gear. Then, with complete smoothness and concentration, Buck let the airplane down onto the glacial snow cover, feeling as if with his own toes the whispering touch of the skis. He throttled back and turned the 185 around a good twenty feet short of the upper crevasse. Cruchot squeezed Buck's shoulder in salute and the two climbers in the back shouted their approval.

Buck left the engine running while the men unloaded and stood with their gear. Cruchot took the HF walkietalkie while Buck shook their mittened hands and pointed thumbs up. Then he returned to the airplane, throttled up to roar a few bounces down the short strip, and pulled up into a semidive down the glacier. The climbers thought they saw him wag his wings once, several miles away.

Each man smiled in the cold wind, ignorant of what lay ahead.

chapter 7

THE SMELL of coffee brought Buck Davis to his seat at the small table by the window. Mary poured for both and sat down in her chair. More than twenty-five years together had surrounded them with both warmth and memories, and the special early coffee each morning was one of the warmest moments of the day.

Mary smiled at her husband as he drank his coffee. How many cups together now? Thousands. And always the smiles were the same. The thoughts were the same. The days might bring tragedy or humor as they see fit, but the morning smiles were always the same. They made sure they were. It was their lodestone for the days and the years. Tied together by something as simple as coffee and a smile in the morning, both felt almost superstitiously that if they could but keep this daily ritual, somehow the combined forces of hazard, age and pain could not harm them. Neither ever voiced these feelings, but both knew nothing short of a village fire would ever interfere.

Early morning. Coffee when the world is dark and quiet. Early morning when the mind is still half submerged in the night's rest.

The quiet time, the together time, waiting for the light to burn across the hills.

They had breakfast and checked the temperature. Buck looked up at the clear sky. He let the dog out. Then they had another cup together.

Buck looked at his watch.

"Time yet?"

Buck nodded. Both slipped into parkas and mukluks and walked through the false porch to the street. Several neighbors came out to join them, glancing at watches and cursing the wind. John Thompson walked over to stand beside Buck and Mary, noticing Mary's smile of pride as he approached.

Buck saw the jet first, high over the village. It didn't vary; it didn't waver. It didn't wag its wings or buzz the South Seas Roadhouse. The neighbors watched the plane and watched Buck and Mary Davis as they stood hand in hand, staring up at the sky.

John Thompson looked at his watch, then back at the jet.

"Just like his dad," he announced. "Two minutes late."

Then the jet was out of sight behind the mountains.

chapter 8

"WANT TO TAKE it in today, Sam?"

Sam Davis looked up from the instruments in front of him and looked at the captain.

"Thanks, Bill. One smooth landing coming up."

"Drop down another two, Sam."

"Right. Down two."

High above the Susitna Flats, Sam Davis looked down on the frozen snaky maze that formed the three mouths of the giant river system.

"There's some good trapping down there, Bill, just waiting for the right person to come along."

"Now how can you tell that from way up here, Sam?"

"Easy. See all those beaver ponds? Full. Which means the dams are intact. Which means the beavers are in each lodge to keep them intact. Which means there are too many beavers."

"Too many beavers?" Bill Ryder asked. "How so?"

"Just a second," Sam replied, picking up the microphone. "Anchorage tower. Central 126 now turning on final. Roger, Anchorage."

Sam put minimal effort on the left rudder and just touched the wheel slightly. Inside the metal machine, a thousand tiny parts responded with the calculated movements of hydraulic accuracy and the giant aircraft began a slight tilt and turn to the left.

"Beavers are stay-at-homes, Bill. Unless they're forced to move by population pressure, they'll stay in the same pond all their lives. If there are too many for the pond, they'll move. Maybe 100 yards. Look down there. Those beavers have occupied every possible pond site in the entire swamp system. If they aren't trapped, and soon, they'll be culled by Mama Nature. By starvation, disease, or both. Probably both. Let's drop the gear."

"Gear down, and locked."

"Roger. Now some flaps."

"Flaps, Captain Sam."

"You know, Bill, I've really enjoyed riding shotgun for you."

"My pleasure, too, Sam. You'll be out of that right-hand seat in no time. You're really good, you know."

"Thanks, Bill. Little more flaps."

"More flaps. Crossing Fire Island."

"Fire Island. Roger. Here we go."

Sam brought the giant jet in smoothly and touched down in Anchorage. He taxied up to the terminal and shut it down.

"Nice landing."

"Our specialty, Bill. I'm buying the coffee."

"You're on. Sam, you learn all that beaver stuff from your family?"

Sam smiled.

"Yeah. Learn a lot of that stuff in my village."

"Kahiltna, right?"

"Kahiltna. Dance and romance center of the Susitna River Valley."

"You pick up all that stuff from your Indian ancestors?"

"Nope. From my dad. Born in Washington state. Blue eyes. Mustache. White man stuff."

"Sorry, Sam. I didn't mean…"

"Forget it, Bill. It's OK."

Over coffee in the pilots' lounge, both men sat in silence thinking of the flight, the weather and other things more personal.

"Hey Sam, Margie and I are having some people over this evening. Nothing fancy. You aren't flying for a while, right? Right. Well, how about coming over?"

"Sure, Bill. That'd be nice. What time?"

"Eight or so."

Sam smiled. "I'll be there."

• • •

Nice, Sam thought. Very nice. Three stories if you count the daylight basement. Bill's house is here in one of these newer Anchorage tracts, built on fill put on top of one of Alaska's oldest muskeg swamps. They think if they charge enough for these houses, buyers will forget the attorney general's warning that in a generation or two this house will be only two stories, and eventually will become part of the swamp. Houses on similar tracts were already sinking several inches per year, but Bill's house stood tall. Sitting here in the truck, Sam thought, I think it is impressive. This is the kind of house that would dare any swamp to try sucking it down, and win.

Walking to the door, hearing the laughter inside, Sam was reminded that this was what he could look forward to one day soon. Full captains can afford these homes. No more apartment. No more hearing neighbors fight and slam doors. Someday one of these homes, and someone to share it, of course. Of course. What woman could turn down a chance to spend a lifetime with Sam Davis, jet jockey and dashing gentleman? OK, Sam, save it for someone who'll appreciate it. Just knock on the door and let's enjoy the party.

"Sam! Come in this house!"

"Hi Bill. Thanks for the invite,"

"Honey, this is Sam Davis. Sam, Margie."

"Hello, Sam. May I get you something? We have just about everything. Of course, if you like, we have soft drinks too."

"A beer will be fine, Margie."

"A beer, coming right up."

"Sam, she didn't mean anything by…"

"By what, Bill?"

"Well, Margie's never been out of Anchorage, really. I mean…"

"Offering soft drinks is what a good hostess should do, Bill, especially to pilots. But what you meant is that the only Native people she sees are down on Fourth Avenue, right?"

"Well, yes, I'm afraid so."

Sam smiled as Margie came back from the kitchen with a beer. "That's OK, Bill. On this particular score, I take after my dad. I can take it or leave it alone. Tonight I think I'll take it."

Why did it rankle? You'd think a man would get used to it after a few years. Of course it was more than myth or prejudice, unfortunately. Most Native people were forced to make a choice between alcoholism and teetotaling. This phenomenon always intrigued Sam and led him to wonder why this was so. Was it because the Native people hadn't any kind of alcohol until the coming of the white man? White men, with several thousand years of drinking behind them, were bound to build a certain tolerance to spirits.

Natural selection, wasn't it? Darwin again. Only the nonalcoholics in history were able to reproduce families and survive, therefore a race of nonalcoholics…But here I am, half Native, half white. Half city boy, half a child of the village. I can handle it. Handle it nicely. But sip gently on that beer, Sam. You've seen too many cousins go under. And you worry a tiny bit, way back there. Will the day come when you find yourself drawn to it? No, man. No, because that will be the last sip of beer I take if I ever feel that way.

What can I talk to these people about? Politics? Really haven't read up much on that. I mean, I know who the governor is, but damned if I know why he is. There is always the weather. There is always the weather.

"Sam, what are you doing hovering in the corner? Come on over here and meet some friends of mine."

Two single girls. Two single men. Secretaries, maybe? No. He'd guess the women were agency people. State or federal. Work for something with initials. Something with initials that depends upon government grants. And the men? Young lawyers. The suits are a giveaway.

"You know, Sam, here, was telling me the most interesting things about beaver dams on the way in today. Fascinating, really."

"Beaver dams, Mr. Davis?"

Mr. Davis. That would make her head of something with initials that writes away for government grants.

"Tell them about it, Sam, will you? I'll go see about the food in the kitchen. Fascinating, really."

"Well, we just saw some beaver lodges along the Su, and I mentioned that they needed trapping to thin them down some."

"Oh my. You mean you could tell from the air?"

"There are certain things you look for."

Maybe I can slip out and help Bill with the food.

"I suppose you were trained for that since you were young, Mr. Davis?"

"To look?"

"At beaver dams, I mean, you know."

"Because I come from a village, you mean?"

"It must be fascinating to actually live in a village. We both work with villages a lot, of course. But it must be very different to actually live there. You believe in hunting and fishing, then, Mr. Davis, subsistence hunting, of course."

"Yes."

"I suppose it is necessary. Seems a shame, somehow, to kill those beautiful animals. But without subsistence hunting, I suppose you'd have a pretty tough time of it."

"Not really. I'm an airline pilot."

"Oh, of course you are! I didn't mean just you, of course, I meant your people, of course."

Sam smiled kindly.

"Will you excuse me? I think I'll go find Bill."

Bill left the kitchen with the food, and left Sam alone with his thoughts, still nursing that beer and staring out at the lights of Anchorage spread out below them.

Anchorage. Los Angeles North. The Great Trap. It gives a person cityness. Here is a city. Take it. Now you don't have to fly to Seattle to go to the symphony or get drunk with millionaires. There is a slight charge, of course. It'll cost just about everything you've got, son. In advance. Privacy first. Then safety. Buy some door locks. Get a color television. Hook onto the cable. Thirty-nine channels. It's all here. Millionaires having coffee at the Captain Crook. Strippers in Spenard. Fights on Fourth Avenue. The cold lights of the Alaska Railroad pulling slowly into the busy night steam of the industrial gulch. The far-off gas flares of the offshore rigs. The cold arctic sting of the wind off the inlet. The distant strobe flashes of jets coming into Elmendorf. The sad detachment of the dancing girls at the Brief Encounter. The desperation of the girls constantly driving up and down Fourth Avenue, looking for trade. And in the alley behind Fourth Avenue, the unseen man who just crawled into a trash bin to sleep his final night in the subzero cold. On the radio the sad, sweet country music of KYAK, the music that takes these people in dreams back to Houston, Keokuk, Charlotte, Twin Falls, Kahiltna. The songs of the simple people sent out to simple people in a complex society. The reminder. The promise. The sweet prayer of simplicity that links some together and divides others into groups. Anchorage is a city, a pretentious city, of course, but a city. And only cities have groups.

"…seems to be enjoying himself, anyway."

"Well, he is rather good looking, don't you think?"

The voices drifted to Sam through the door to the hallway, and were all the sadder to him because of the genuine sincerity they held. "You should hear Margie, about how she tried to find, you know, someone for him. It was really comical. I mean, you see Native girls every day downtown, but when you need one…well…"

"We shouldn't be talking like this. He is nice."

"Lots of them are, you know."

Sam made his excuses and drove toward town.

What the hell am I doing at the Montana Club? Deafening noise. Tony and the band. Why do I want to dance tonight? Why do I want the noise, the shouting?

"Beer please."

"What?"

Sam shouted. "Beer!"

"Sure, pal. You got the money? Let's see it."

Sam sat at the long bar, listening to the nasal mumbled words of the band. They had long ago forgotten the words to all but the most recent tunes, and those wouldn't last long. Whatever else the Montana Club might be, it is vibrant. There is always a certain touch of danger in going there, as fights are not an uncommon occurrence. Not more often than several times each night.

"Sammy! It's Sammy, isn't it? Shore it is!"

"Hello, Chester. How you been?"

"Drunk, Sam, drunk. Howsa folks?"

"Just fine, Chester. Don't see you up home much anymore."

"Home? Ha, ha."

Chester broke into a coughing fit, then smiled at Sam. "This's home, Sam. Buy me beer, huh? Buy me beer."

"I think you've already had enough, Chester."

"Sam, we cousins, or what, right? Buy me beer."

"What have you been doing for money, Chet?"

"Got new job, Sam. New job. Good one. Buy me beer."

"What are you doing?"

"I'm a Native, Sam."

"Well, of course."

"Perfessional, Sam, I'm a perfessional Native. Money, too."

"A professional Native. What's that?"

Chester laughed and went into another coughing fit.

"Stories. Legendary stories. Legends. Story legends. All that stuff. Sam, buy me beer."

"OK, just one. What stories?"

Chester chuckled. Then he whispered.

"I make 'em up. Great stories. Then I tell the ladies, and they put them on a tape recorder for Washington, D.C., and they get money from a grant and pay me. Wanna hear one? I call it 'The Day the Weasel Discovered Bread.'"

"I never heard that one, Chester."

"Neither did I. But I ran out of raven stories. Buy me 'nother beer."

"Why don't you go back to the village, Chester? You have family there, and friends."

"Not me. Nossir. Gonna be famous. Took my picture. 'Legendary storyteller,' they call me. Buy me beer, Sam."

"No more."

"You my cousin or what? I mean what the hell. You my cousin or what? Come on, Sam, buy me beer."

"I'm going home, Chester. See you around."

"Hey, good Sam. I'll go with you. You got beer at home? I'll sleep onna couch, Sam."

"Wrong, Chester. I'm going to Kahiltna."

"Gonna go to Kahiltna? Be an Indian, huh, Sam? Gonna go back to the village, be a big Indian! Well, you're nothin', Sam. Hear me, you're nothin'! Go back and be a big Native Indian. See what, well, you're nothin', go home."

"Good night, Chet. I'm going."

"Sam, wait. Just buy me beer, huh? Just one beer, huh, Sam? Tell you story Sam, tell you story."

Sam walked out into the cold wind off the inlet and headed for his truck. It must have been the wind that made his eyes water.

chapter 9

FRANK GRANGER poured himself a cup of coffee and walked upstairs to his room in the South Seas. He turned on the light, sipped his coffee, then sat down at his desk with a fresh piece of paper.

Dear Candy:

It's quiet tonight, here in my room, and I'm once again thinking of you, wondering what you're doing tonight, and hoping you are well.

These months we've been writing have been the happiest of my life, and I hope they'll continue. When you wrote me, out of the blue like that, I didn't know what to think, but time, and your letters, have brought me to know you so very well. We're so very different, Candy, in a lot of ways. My world is a constantly changing one of mud, snow, rain and bugs, offset with wonderful people who live their lives and then die. But they find in their brief span of time here a special meaning, and I guess I find a special meaning, too, of my own. To answer your question, no, I don't plan to live Outside again. Not for any reason, I'm afraid. Ten years ago I went back to my boyhood home in Illinois, but it wasn't the same. My brother has the farm, of course, and he and his wife told me I would always have a home there. But it is his farm now, not ours. I discovered I don't speak the same language as people in Illinois, either. I don't speak a word of farm economics, and they think grizzly bears live on television, or were killed off a hundred years ago. I stayed a week, and couldn't sleep the entire time.

You also asked me about coming up for a visit, and as much as I'd like that, I think it's best that you don't. Let me explain, Candy, as I would not like to hurt you in any way.

Granger stood and walked to the window and looked down on the empty snow-covered street and across it to the airplanes shrouded in wing covers and engine blankets. The gleam from the single yard light brought back memories of campfires in the snow, bleak days of breaking trail in front of the dog team, the misty glow of lights across the valley that marked the diggings of neighboring gold miners. He seemed to see the endless ebb and flow of life in the village as he watched. The years, the people, the laughs, the sorrows, the deaths, the weddings—all seemed to file by, smile their smile, shed their tear, then leave. Winter was the magic time, Frank reflected. This is what Alaska was all about. In spring there are only memories and promises, summer is the work time of long days and nonexistent nights, and fall is the time of the hunt, of expectation and challenge. Winter is Alaska. Tourists are gone, leaving the giant country to those who love it. Winter is a time of legends, of heroic deeds that go unheralded by the world, of friendships, stories and occasional tragedy. Winter in Kahiltna is a time of introspection, a time to ask oneself the important questions. A time to think. A time to read. A time for ideas.

Winter is Alaska. This is when the country lives up to its billing. If Alaskans were to be honest with themselves, winter is why they came. It is the grand testing time, when minds and nerves and bodies are tested against the cold, the darkness, the loneliness. This is when Alaskans secretly look at the heavens and exult in daring the elements to do their worst. They are up to it. The ultimate victory is the return of the sun come breakup, but with it comes a sadness, a mourning of the passing of a worthy adversary.

Frank Granger thought about Candy with regrets. She was a woman, and such a woman! But this is Alaska, and Alaska ate women. It took their cheerfulness, their hopes, and occasionally, their lives. It is a rare woman who can enjoy the Alaska life, as Alaska tends to belittle the things women find dear. An Alaska winter scoffs at party clothes, hair styles and jewelry. There is simply too much real living going on to be bothered with trivialities. Shopping becomes a necessity, not an art. The surface niceties of civilization are washed away to make room for basics, and few women can be satisfied for long with only heat, shelter, food and love.

What began as a village joke was now serious business to Frank. He still didn't know who submitted his name to the matchmaking club, but it did seem a good joke. Frank went along with it at first, making up rather wild stories for the women who wrote to him. When these were shared with the village, another legend was born. The first few months found Frank Granger sending off duplicate letters to these lonely women, with a spare copy posted on the South Seas bulletin board for the entertainment of the village in general. Then came Candy's first letter. Within a week, Frank wrote a final letter to the others, falsely claiming he had gotten married, and there was left only Candy.

Candy's first letter had touched his heart with its innocence and wonder. Although he knew she was roughly his age, there was a tenderness about it that could not be trifled with. He found a certain oneness with this woman, whose photograph he had never even seen. As months rolled by, Frank began to live every day for eleven in the morning, when the mail would be sorted and delivered to the boxes. It was, in a way, a double life. Here was a woman who was willing to listen to the most trivial things he had to say. She remembered each of them in the next letter, and asked questions that were probing without being pushy. Frank found something deep within him that leaped at this chance. He was no writer, and deep philosophies were not the usual subject of conversation with his rough-booted friends downstairs. Candy's letters appealed to the poet in Frank, and through writing her, he began to see with more than his eyes. He looked at things with a new sensitivity, asking himself how best to explain the new things occurring in the village to Candy.

Candy. How well he knew her! She never wrote about the everyday, and in fact, he didn't know whether she lived in a house or apartment. She never wrote of what she did during the day, or the people she met. She was, at once, deeply interested in Frank's people, and secretive about her own. His questions about her life had been cleverly sidestepped, but he had learned about her. He could see Candy clearly. Her cares for others were clear. She was a partner to Frank in many ways. They had this to share. In a way, it was a marriage, a good marriage. It was the secret time of day lovers shared when they were at rest and talked about their souls and fears and feelings. Frank sometimes wondered what he'd do if she stopped writing to him, and a sudden panic made his heart pound. It would be like taking away his sight, and he forced himself to put all thoughts of discontinuing the correspondence from his mind. The marriage he had shied away from all these years was here in its purest form. All the intimacy without the dirty dishes. All the friendship without the arguments.

This mailbox relationship had delicacy, intimacy and strength, and was therefore a fragile thing. Frank took longer to write Candy's letters these days, as he didn't want anything to interrupt the correspondence. As finicky as he was about any possible misunderstandings coming between them, their relationship had ironically grown to a point of frankness that startled him. Frank was able to unburden himself of his deepest secrets and cares because he would never be any closer to Candy than he was now. It is almost like writing a diary that writes back, he thought. Distance and differences meant they were safe in opening up their most intimate thoughts. Honesty without the need for diplomacy. Yet this diary responded, with a warmth he had never cared to seek in a woman. It made for a perplexing and delicious situation.

Frank sat down at his desk again and continued writing.

Alaska is man's country, dear, and I don't mean to sound like a chauvinist. Of course, there are women here, as well. Good ones, too. It's just that it takes a certain type of woman to make a life here, and I can tell from your letters that you are much too sensitive to be happy in such a rough land. And so, I think it is best that you not come up. At least, not right now. Maybe some summer or early fall when the weather's nice we can arrange for a visit.

Candy, I might as well admit I'm afraid of what a visit might do to us. This country is not as you picture it, I'm sure, and it can be quite inhospitable. An awful lot of it around here is muskeg swamp, which harbors uncounted millions of mosquitoes each summer. Most of the trees are nothing to write home about, although in some areas they grow quite large. The winters are cold and long. Very long. Snow lies on the ground a full six months of the year, and the river and creeks are frozen for five of those months, in an average year.

I don't think it's the country that scares me about your visit, though. Sweet girl, I'm an old man, and not very pretty. I'm tall and bony and kind of sticklike all over. Some of my friends say that if I stood sideways and stuck out my tongue, I'd look like a zipper.

I guess it's just the fear that meeting me in person may be a real disappointment. Not that I've necessarily painted myself to be anything but what I am, but there are bound to be differences between us. I'm really too old and set in my ways to consider any lasting relationship, which in people of our age translates into marriage. It would find us, I'm afraid, always waiting for that something, that insurmountable problem, that would drive us apart. And that, dear one, is something I know I couldn't handle. And there is one other thing.

The knock on the door interrupted Frank Granger's writing. "Come on in."

It was Hemingway Jones. "Hope I'm not interrupting you, Frank."

"Yes you are, but I'm glad of it, Hemingway. Sit down and take a load off."

"Another letter to Candy?"

"Yes." Frank looked slightly embarrassed. "You'd think she'd get tired of me after all these months."

"Must be getting serious, Frank."

"Just how serious can a man get when he hasn't even met a woman? I don't even know what she looks like."

"Seems to me that may not be the most important thing."

Frank looked at Hemingway. "Sometimes you show wisdom far

beyond your years. How old are you?"

"Twenty-eight."

"Twenty-eight! God!"

"Frank, I need your advice about something."

Frank loaded his battered pipe and lit it. "Shoot."

"Well, you know I've been trying to write stories for quite a while now."

Frank nodded and blew out some smoke.

"Well, frankly I'm getting nowhere fast. Minnie suggested I write about Alaska and the people here."

"That's good advice."

"That's how I figure it, too. Well, you know, I've been here, in the South Seas, practically the entire time I've lived in Alaska. All I know of Alaska is what I hear downstairs in the bar."

Frank smiled. "Some of it is actually true, you know."

"I know. But I haven't lived in the Bush myself. I need to get the feel of the country. I don't want to write about something I know nothing about. Know what I mean?"

"Sure do. Especially when writing about Alaska. Any real sourdough can spot a phony in the first few pages."

"That's right. So I want to take a few days and go stay in the Bush, if it's OK with you."

"Sure, that's hunky-dory. Call it my contribution to Alaska literature. Where will you go?"

"That's the other thing, Frank. I thought maybe you could suggest some place. I mean, where I wouldn't bother anyone."

Frank scratched his head and smoked a while.

"Know just the place. Swenson's cabin. Know where it is?"

Hemingway shook his head.

"Cross the river and up about three miles. You'll round a bend with lots of driftwood piled up. Turn back in there, and the cabin is right at the base of a bluff. Maybe quarter of a mile from the river. Ice should be safe by now, but go slow, and wear snowshoes."

"Was that the guy who hated airplanes?"

Frank smiled. "I see you've heard the stories. Yes, that's the guy. Don't know just how much is there, so take enough stuff so you can camp out if you have to. Got a Woods Four-Star bag in the closet, there. Take it along when you get ready to go."

"Thanks, Frank."

"Hemingway, you ever do this before?"

"Not in winter."

"Take lots of matches, and an ax. Of course, trapper Swenson's place is only three miles from here, so you could get out in a hurry if something happened, but don't take any chances. If you take more than you need, you'll never need it. At least, that has always seemed to be true."

"Thanks."

"My outdoor stuff is in the big closet. Sleeping bag, pack frame, cooking gear, snowshoes. Take 'em."

"Thanks a lot, Frank. I'll take good care of them."

"OK, kid," Frank grinned as Hemingway walked to the door, "stay warm and have fun."

Hemingway grinned and left Frank sitting there smiling and shaking his head. He finished his pipe slowly and closed his eyes and heard the country music coming up from the jukebox. The smile lines were etched deep around his eyes as he thought about Hemingway Jones, and all the many hundreds of others.

I hope he finds it, thought Frank. Whatever it is that sends him out into the winter woods, I hope he finds it. He's a good boy. No. A good man, by golly. There have been so many go out into the winter woods, looking for it. Peace, whatever it is. Challenge, maybe. Peace, I think. And maybe just a little curiosity about themselves and how good they are. A few found death out there, but maybe that's what they were looking for, too.

I went once, too. Once? Hell, I went once and again and again and again for years, who am I kidding? Did I find it? Well, did I, or didn't I? Yes, I guess I found it. I found me, and that's what I was looking for. I met Frank Granger out in the woods and found he was an all-right guy. Liked him, truth be known. Went back for enough visits, I did. Wonder if old Frank is still out there? And why am I smiling at that? You know, one of these days I'll just go back out there for a visit. Will I, really? Yes, by God, I will. Because it's still there, and I'm here, and I'll do it. That's something Candy could never understand.

Frank picked up his letter and read the last line.

"And there is one other thing..."

He tapped out his pipe into the ashtray and bent once more to his work.

> ...that must be considered. I guess the biggest thing women hate about the Bush is the competition. You see, Candy, the wilderness is a temptress, a siren that can reach into the hearts of cities all over the world and seduce those men who have seen her. Women tend to get jealous of this country, and a woman who would care for me would find the same problem, I'm afraid. I'm at the age now where gentle country should appeal to me. Men my age are entitled to sit on a

porch somewhere and smell honeysuckle and listen to the crickets. I couldn't do it, sweet girl. I love this country, I confess. I love the subtle shades of color the mountain takes on in late afternoon. I love the chilling howl of the wolf on the hunt. I love even the uncertainty of life itself here, as it tends to intensify the living of each day, and fill a man with thankfulness at the end of it.

Please believe me when I tell you that this is not any form of brush-off, because you are dear to me. It's just that I've been having this love affair for more than fifty years, and it's got me forever. I'll die here, Candy, and ask for nothing more than to be a small part of this country and the vibrant way of life it shelters.

I didn't mean to go off at the mouth so much tonight, my dear, but I owe you honesty, and you got it. That'll be enough for tonight. My old eyes are getting tired.

If I were there tonight, I'd tuck you in and give you a sneaky little kiss. Maybe when you close your eyes tonight you'll hear me sneak in for that kiss. Don't scream, dear one, for it's just this harmless old-timer who cares a lot for you.

Yours with sincerest affection,
Frank.

chapter 10

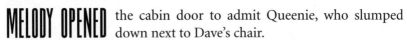

MELODY OPENED the cabin door to admit Queenie, who slumped down next to Dave's chair.

"What's the matter, girl? Rabbits just too fast for you yet?"

"I think she ought to stay home for a while, Dave, until she feels stronger."

"Hear that, Queenie? Sounds like you've been grounded."

Dave smiled at the dog and rubbed her ears. The young trapper pulled on parka and mittens and kissed his pretty wife long and then again.

"Maybe today will be a good day," he whispered.

"Sure it will. Maybe we need more traps."

"What we need around here is a more skillful trapper, I'm afraid."

"You'll do just fine, thank you."

"Have it your way, ma'am," he said, bowing low.

"Honey…be careful."

He winked at her and left the cabin. He could hear Queenie whining as he strapped on the snowshoes and started up the hill behind the cabin.

The bear had experienced good years: beautiful summers and autumns when the living was easy and the winter sleep slipped in quietly and full.

Things had changed.

There is a desperation that comes on a grizzly bear with age. When a bear has won his battles, reproduced his strength with another, taken his share of game: then the kindness Nature owes a completed job is a swift death. As he had taken his share of moose and caribou quickly and surely, the bear deserved to go as quickly as the whisper-strike of the hunter's bullet, or the quick crush of a younger bear.

But now the bear was old, and age brought with it indignities that are unseemly to wild creatures. The teeth that had crushed the life from so many were now worn knobs. The split-second reflex of muscle that could have brought down the swiftest race horse had slackened to a lumbering shuffle through the snow. His silver-streaked hide, once shiny and rolling with muscle, now hung in dull folds over the remnant of his body. Food was hard to catch.

There hadn't been enough food this fall to allow the bear to go to ground. Within his brain ran two urgent thoughts. He was burning with the desire to eat and sleep, and it was contradicted by the passion to avoid the wolves. Once he was asleep in a den, neither the bravest nor hungriest of wolves would dare dig him up. They could not tell from the outside of the den that this was an old bear. It was simply a bear. His scent and his wide track were the only remnants now that said this was once a prince of the tundra.

If wolves caught him in deep snow, he would be surrounded and nipped until his strength left. His tender parts would be eaten even before life had left his body. It was an indignity reserved for those who survived beyond their time.

So the bear shuffled along the windblown ridge where the snow was thinnest, following the only sensory organ left to him in full: his nose. Up ahead was blood. That it was blood from a ptarmigan sprinkled on a marten set, he couldn't know. Perhaps years ago that message would have penetrated to his hunting brain. But time had slowed the flow of information into the most basic parts. Where there was blood there was meat. Where there was meat, he must go. He must eat, then sleep.

The bear shuffled along the ridge slowly, heading for Dave's trap line.

• • •

The first set on the ridge had a few interested tracks around it, but there were no takers. Dave looked long at the scene, and tried to reconstruct the happenings. Read the sign and see what went wrong, he told himself. Where did the marten first suspect this was a set? Right there. Then he circled around to this knob to take a closer look. Dave was proud of his new possession of this age-old trapper's skill, learned day by day by looking at the impressions of feet in snow and deciphering track by track what transpired.

But to get so close and not score was disheartening. It wasn't so much the money, Dave had to admit. The money from the fur would help, of course, but Dave was a cautious man, and had planned to spend the first winter simply learning to trap. It was more than that. It was the slap in the face the wary marten had given him. The animal had pranced within inches of the traps and scorned the best efforts of the trapper.

In the past weeks, Dave had learned more than trapping; he had learned the delicious anticipation felt by generations of trappers and prospectors. Snowshoeing through the forest was in itself a way of life, but when it coupled with the anticipation of rounding the next curve of trees, alert eyes searching for that first sign of fur, the frenzy of the animal's last minutes in the traps before it succumbed to the cold, that's what kept him going. It was the same with prospectors. That is why so many are content simply to locate the gold and let others do the work of mining it. It was the thrill of finding it, of working with and against Nature, of plotting his skills against those around him and winning.

The bear jumped him on the third trap.

There hadn't been warning enough to get out the pistol. There was just this crushing weight and the frenzied attack. He thrashed in the snow in the arctic gear, making futile attempts to fend off teeth. Each time he fought, the bear roared and bit. The first attack opened skin on Dave's face. The second laid the skin back over his eyes. He could no longer see clearly. It wasn't until the calm between attacks that he heard the rumbling over him and realized he was in the grip of a bear.

He had got between the bear and the dead ptarmigan, which was unforgivable. The bear looked down at the quivering hunk beneath his weight. Dave tried holding his breath. The pain of the torn flesh had not yet reached his brain, and the natural instincts now emerged cautiously and told him to lie still.

It worked.

After a few more bites to Dave's shoulders, the old grizzly stepped off Dave's back, carefully picked up the dead ptarmigan and walked away.

It was minutes before Dave moved. He didn't feel the cold, but he began to feel the pain. His ears listened for the bear. There was silence for long minutes, then Dave heard the grunting down in the creek bed, and he tried to see.

The world was a crazy red. When he sat up the pain began. A moan escaped him, but he instantly silenced himself and swung his head to see whether the bear understood the sound.

Thinking methodically, he moved there on the snow until he was certain no bones were broken, then pulled himself slowly erect by clinging to an alder. Feeling his way down the packed back trail, he shuffled step after step toward the cabin. It wasn't far. Just a lifetime away. A lifetime of victory and defeat. He was alive, and he had been beaten by the world.

Through the red-pained haze he shuffled as the bear had shuffled, feeling his way along the packed trail, trying to close out the pain.

He knew he was home only by the frantic barking of Queenie, the slamming of the cabin door and Melody's screams.

Dave was lying in his bed. He felt cold water on what was left of his face. Melody's eyes focused on the face before her, but her brain mercifully shut out the sight. She worked methodically to stop the major bleeding.

"The neighbors have a radio. I'll go call."

Dave shook his head.

"Bear…"

"I know, darling. But I must go. Don't move until I'm back. Promise me? DAVE! Promise me?"

Dave nodded painfully, his thoughts jumbled and swimming and blurred.

He started to sit up, but Melody pushed him back down. He said, "Take Queenie."

Melody said she would, then dressed for the cold and left the cabin.

Dave tried everything to ignore the pain during those hours. He tried to will the pain away. He fought the pain, as if by doing so he could conquer it. He told himself that if there was pain, at least there was life. If life continues, the pain will be forced to stop eventually.

But the pain became heavier and heavier with the hours. It began with the face, but it soon spread to the shoulders where the heavier bites had been made. It roamed around his body like a snake looking for opportunities. It found bruises where the bear's weight and claws had done minor damage, and set up outposts in these places, adding to the total weight.

Thinking was becoming very difficult. Dave's premise that pain could be ignored was faulty, his faith that where there is life the pain must leave was wrong. There was still life, but the pain grew worse. It became like the air during a cold snap. It had a weight and a pressure and a substance of its own. It was like a cancerous growth, spreading rapidly, taking over his body, making him doubt the most deep-seated feelings of his being.

He opened his eyes to search for an answer to the pain. Through a red haze he searched, looking for a last opportunity to win the battle.

Through the unfocused haze, Dave saw the big rifle hanging over the door. He stared at it and tried to look through it. He tried to go over each of its actions and weigh the possibilities.

When he tried to reach it, the pain clubbed him into unconsciousness.

He awoke briefly as hands moved over him, and deft fingers probed his face. He later remembered only the whopping of the rotors as the helicopter lifted from the lake, but he knew the cool softness of Melody's hand on his during the flight.

chapter 11

BUCK DAVIS saw the helicopter rise out of the vastness of the lake system, and turned to 121.5, the emergency frequency.
"Rescue chopper, rescue chopper, this is 44952 Lima."
"Hello, Buck. Headed for the mountain?"
"Roger, making an airdrop to those climbers. You have Dave with you?"
"Roger."
"How's he doing?"
"He'll make it, Buck."
"Thank you, boys. I'm clear."

・・・

Cruchot rested high on the ridge. Amateurs. Almost always they're amateurs, thought Cruchot. Below him the nylon rope led down to Hunter as he negotiated the chimney. The third climber, Morris, rested at the foot of the chimney, winded.
"What's the matter, Big Mo?" Hunter called down good naturedly. "Eat too much of my cooking this morning?"
"I'll be fine, son. Just need a break."
A break! Cruchot spat and turned his head away from his companions. Far up the peak stretched, rock and ice surrounded by sky. At this rate they wouldn't make the summit. One day behind schedule now. Any more slack climbing habits like this, and they would be two days behind schedule. Three-day weather allowance on food, which means no cushion.
Amateurs!
Buck maintained a fast airspeed when he came close to the Comb. The plane was tossed by the wind, but he had gauged it accurately, and the craft stayed well away from the grip of rocks and ice.
He spotted the climbers on the second pass. They were lower than he had anticipated, but he chalked that up to this being a winter climb. They were in a bad spot for an airdrop, but just 100 yards farther up the Comb was a small hollow in the glacier. The timing would be tricky. The hollow was about ten yards across. He would have to come in fast from the east.
He flew low over the climbers and watched Cruchot stare back with

frost-covered faceplate and goggles and wave one hand, the signal that all was fine with the team. Buck wagged his wings when he was clear of the ridge and circled for the drop.

Over the years, Buck had become famous for his pinpoint "bombing" on airdrops around Kahiltna. He had been a bit more conservative for the past several years, though, since one airdrop that hadn't gone according to plan. Proudly proclaiming "service right to your front door," Buck had dropped a canned ham right through Wild Bill Murphy's front porch.

This drop on the mountain was another thing, though. The face on the Comb was steep. If he misjudged his drop, the sacks would go plummeting down the slope and do the climbers no good. If he misjudged his approach, he would become part of the mountain for eternity.

Turning into the strong headwind, Buck pulled partial flaps for stability and advanced the throttle. The door was cracked, and Buck held one corner of the first gunnysack out the door, guiding the plane with his left. The wind did not gust, and the plane came in as stable as an ocean liner above the target.

Buck released the sack and saw it fall the fifty feet to strike the outer edge of the hollow. It had missed falling down the glacier by three feet.

"Have to drop a little sooner," Buck said to himself, and swung around for the next two drops. The second drop put the sack in the exact center of the hollow. On the last run, the third sack landed on the second sack and rolled off to become the closest of neighbors.

"You can sleep tonight, your bomber squadron's awake," Buck mumbled, pleased with the work.

The plane swung out, wagged its wings and headed back for the village.

Buck looked back at the mountain and the three specks clinging to it. He half-waved his hand at them, pulled the harmonica from his pocket and began to play.

The three climbers listened as the roar of the plane blended into the windy hush of the canyon. They thought about what they had just seen, and each was quiet with his own thoughts. It would perhaps be the last thing they agreed on.

chapter 12

WHEN JOHN THOMPSON and Frank Granger walked into the bar, they stopped at the sight, then circled the bandaged figure, looking at each other. One eye showed through the bandages.

"Well, John, it's sitting next to Melody," Frank said. "What do you suppose it is?"

"Could be Dave under there, Frank. What do you think?"

"That you in there, Dave?"

The swathed head nodded.

Frank took a close look and said, "They missed a place right over here, Dave. I can still see some skin."

The figure chuckled, but the laughing hurt, and Granger apologized.

"Can you drink a beer?"

Dave pointed to a small mouth opening and said yes in a weak voice.

"Hemingway!" Granger shouted. "One beer and a long straw!"

John looked over at Melody.

"You kids going back out to the lake this winter?"

"Of course," she said. "That's our home."

John Thompson and Frank Granger joined the couple at their table.

How fortunate, Thompson thought. Their grizzly came in solid form and they survived. Most bush people aren't that lucky. When people move up here, the one thing they fear is the attack of a grizzly bear. Dave here will carry the scars of that battle for the rest of his life, but they are real scars, visible scars, the kind people look at and say, "There's a person who has gone through something terrible and survived."

But the grizzlies that defeat most people up here are the bears of adversity and fear.

There is the bear of hunger, which attacks people who do not prepare adequately. And the grizzly that gnaws at the mind of the person who knows he was foolish. There is the old silvertip of cabin fever, when marriages go under, minds are shattered into so much frozen flotsam, and the defeated then head for the city lights with the old sow grizzly knowledge of failure to eat away at their vitals for the rest of their lives.

And, thought John, the cruelest bears of all are those that leave the inner scars of defeat, rather than the outer scars of victory. The biting, clawing knowledge that what we thought we were, we aren't. What we wanted to be, we can't.

"John? You all right?"

"Yes, Missy, I'm just fine," he smiled at Melody. "I was just thinking of ordering another beer for everyone."

"That's what I call a fine thought," grinned Frank.

"You know something, kids?" John said with a smile. "You are going to make it just fine. Just fine."

The arrival of a car outside turned heads, and there was a shout of laughter when they saw Buck park the station wagon and emerge with Pete Kelly and Siwash Simmons in tow.

Kelly looked around. "You fellas got a soft chair for a dyin' man?"

"Kelly here had them nurses buying flowers for him down there at the hospital," Simmons said, "and I thought the doctors was going to pay us to haul him out of there."

"Laugh if you will, Simmons, laugh if you will. You aren't laughing at Dave there, now, are you? Of course not! Hi, Dave. How you doing? Good. Now Simmons here has sympathy for you because you got bandages. But me? It's my innards that are all torn up. That's why I'm a convalescent, the nurses said. Anybody got a lap robe?"

"A what?" asked Granger.

"A lap robe. A lap robe. Is that so difficult to understand? Hell, all convalescents have to have lap robes, you know that."

"Are convalescents allowed to have a beer?" Frank Granger asked.

"No beer. The doctor said no beer. Nothing but medication."

"You bring your medication bottle, Pete?"

"Got it right here, but it's empty."

"Hemingway! Would you kindly fill this prescription with medication for Kahiltna's resident convalescent?"

"Such is the elixir of life," muttered Hemingway, taking the empty bottle behind the bar and returning with it filled.

"Just in time, too," Pete said, taking a stiff belt.

Siwash Simmons ordered a beer and sat at the bar, gesturing over his shoulder toward Kelly. "I've known this man for nearly forty years, and I've never known him to contradict a doctor's orders. In fact, I've known him to stay medicated for three days at a stretch."

"What brings you out of the hills this time of year, Si?" Frank asked.

"Needed some new clothes. Got this jacket for forty bucks. New, too. Needed some grub. Dogs needed shots. Pete needed a wet nurse…"

"Wet nurse! Why…"

"Easy, old timer," Buck laughed. "You're just sore 'cause you didn't get a new jacket like your partner."

"That is a beautiful jacket," Pete admitted. "And you know it looks like just the kind of jacket a convalescent needs to bring him back to health and vitality."

"Fat chance!" Siwash said. "Buy your own jacket."

"Selfish booger, ain't he?" said Pete.

Conversation and laughter continued in the South Seas, but outside the weather was dull. The cloud cover had returned, insulating the land and warming the air but muting the stark black and white of the village to a somber gray. The sky was a uniform yellow-gray. The mood soon fell on the crowd in the South Seas Roadhouse, and each was quiet with his own thoughts. Minnie Hunter looked out the window of the trading post across the square and made a mental note to order more wool socks.

John Thompson got up from the table, stretched and silently walked out the door of the roadhouse. He walked to his cabin across the street, past the silent airplanes, and went into the whitewashed log structure.

He washed his face meticulously, combed his hair with Vitalis, and admired his handiwork. He changed to a clean wool shirt and walked to the old but powerful stereo set on the shelf. Selecting a long-playing polka album, he turned up the volume to full blast, opened the doors and windows of his cabin, and walked out.

The blaring accordion and tuba music streaked out of the cabin and infiltrated every hidden crack in the village. Heads popped out of cabins, smiled and popped back in. John Thompson was on the loose again, and heaven knows what would happen.

John walked with the determination of a general about to enter the gates of Rome, a smile curling on his reddish face. He walked straight to the door of the trading post, and emerged dragging Minnie Hunter, who was desperately trying to rid herself of her work apron.

In the street, between the airplanes and the parked cars, John Thompson and Minnie Hunter hopped around on the hard snow surface in a grand polka. Oblivious of others, they continued through two polkas before another couple joined them. The reprobates in the South Seas emerged and formed a dance-hall wall. Dave and Melody hugged each other and swayed back and forth.

As if the blaring music weren't enough, the mukluk telegraph of the northern people swept the village with the news. The street filled with dancers while the others clapped in time to the music.

Mitten slapped mitten as the grins shone from under the parka hoods, and the rollicking dance went on. Kelly shared some of his medication with Siwash as they watched the dancers.

When exhausted dancers shouted for beer, Hemingway Jones and Buck Davis brought several cases out of the South Seas. Harry Pete brought a washtub full of caribou sausage, and a full-blown midwinter outdoor party was in progress.

Several hours later the onlookers were in a quandary. It was too warm to freeze to death, but too cold to just stand there watching the dancers. No one would consider going indoors to warm up, so even the more decrepit among the villagers began dancing.

After much mutual medication, Siwash Simmons turned to his partner.

"Mr. Kelly, may I have the pleasure of this dance?"

"Wearing that new jacket of yours, I suppose, Simmons. Wouldn't that be a thing to show the neighbors. Here you are, hale and hearty, wearing a brand-new forty-dollar jacket, and here's your dance partner, virtually at death's door, in just an old faded parka. You should be ashamed of yourself!"

Siwash thought a minute.

"Tell you what, Kelly. You wear my new jacket, and I'll wear your old parka, and we'll hop around and keep warm."

Pete Kelly pulled off his parka and reached for the new jacket.

"I lead," he said.

The dancers agreed that Pete Kelly had found some reserve of strength that evening. As darkness fell, and pickups were pulled around the dance area to illuminate it with headlights, Kelly was doing his share of polka dancing, with occasional moments of medication thrown in.

He flashed Siwash's new jacket as would a peacock his tail, and when the cloud cover disappeared around midnight, leaving Kahiltna in numbing cold, Pete was still in drunken possession of the jacket. He wore it in the early hours of morning, as he climbed the steep staircase of the South Seas Roadhouse to his room.

"No appreciation for a sick man," he mumbled, pausing for a quick refill of his medication. "Man'd think nobody cared any more for his neighbor. Helluva world any more."

In his room, he staggered upright to look at himself in the bureau mirror. Zipping up the jacket to the throat, he thought that, if he died this instant, he would at least make a handsome corpse.

He chuckled, medicated himself for the night, and stretched out on the bed.

Folding his arms funereally across his chest, he said "Why, a man as sick as I am might even die tonight, but what would they care, anyhow?"

He smiled at himself, winked an eye at the bottle of medication, and closed his eyes. His heart stopped an hour later.

• • •

They were forced to put Pete in an old snowmachine crate, but it didn't matter. Any formal burial arrangements would have to wait until after breakup.

It was a sad and silent cortege that carried the makeshift casket down the steep steps of the South Seas Roadhouse next morning and out into the street. Villagers waited outside, and followed silently as the state trooper, Bob Mackin, led the way across the village square to the storage shed.

Hemingway looked across the box at Buck Davis on the other side.

"I didn't think he was that sick."

"I don't think he was, until he died," Buck said.

This made Hemingway feel better.

The trooper opened the shed and the men stacked Pete on some boxes. Several noted that the makeshift casket said, "Contents: Fun for the whole family in winter."

Siwash snickered, then snuffled. The men stood around the casket and threw back their parka hoods in respect. The day was bitter cold, and their breath stuck to the metal ceiling like stalactites of frost.

Trooper Macklin was the first to speak.

"I wrote a letter this morning to Pete's niece."

There were nods of approval around the casket.

"We ought to have a proper send-off," Frank said quietly.

"In the spring," said Buck.

"In the spring," agreed Frank.

Hemingway stared at the casket and looked around nervously, waiting for someone to say something. Finally he cleared his throat.

"I'd like to say something for Pete that Shakespeare wrote."

"That'd be nice," Siwash said.

Hemingway straightened up, standing tall and looking toward the horizon. He cleared his throat, then recited,

"Fear no more the heat of the sun,
nor the furious winter's rages;
Thou thy worldly task hast done,
Home art gone, and taken thy wages.
 Golden lads and girls all must,
as chimney-sweepers come to dust."

They all looked silently at the young man who had so passionately uttered these words. They all smiled and approved. Some even understood.

Siwash said, "I knew Pete Kelly as well as anyone. He was cranky and maybe a little crazy sometimes. He was a lousy housekeeper, and he always thought he was sick. But then again, there was never a time he didn't have a piece of candy for a child, and I never knew him to be mean to a dog."

"Neither did I."

"Me neither."

"That's right."

Hemingway, pleased at the reception of his recitation, tried again.

"An actor frets and struts…"

"Yeah, yeah, I know," said Siwash Simmons, wiping away tears, "but most of them don't do it in their partner's new forty-dollar jacket."

chapter 13

THERE FOLLOWED several days of intense cold. The biting snap of a "drop" is, like a snowstorm, a cohesive force in a small village. The villagers may be of different races, have different hobbies and earn their livings in different ways, but the weather and the solitude tie each to each. It is always the common denominator with peoples of the North, and when all else fails, the weather will come through as a conversation piece.

But it is more than that. The weather, in its ever-changing moods, gives one a brotherly feeling toward his neighbor. When it is twenty below zero, it is twenty below zero for the next man too. Just as in a major disaster, people show concern and love for total strangers; the severity of the weather brings people together in the North.

Snowstorms tend to keep people inside their cabins, watching the fire and the snow, but the intense cold stimulates visiting. On the cold days, each cabin has a huge pot of coffee. In most homes, women—or men who like to think they can get along without women—bake cookies or fry doughnuts. It is a time of conversations, of recalling other cold snaps, of monologues that invariably begin, "Why, I can remember one time it was so cold that I actually saw..."

Sam Davis walked down the street, interrupting an argument between two dogs as he went. He saw the heavy steam pouring from the stovepipes and heater vents of each house, and liked it. There was something invigorating about the deep cold, as if to live in it and live through it was a challenge. Each cold day's end was a victory for each of the people.

Harry Pete was at home when Sam arrived, and in the golden light thrown by the windows, he could see the Pete children playing in the small house.

After hugs from the children, Sam poured himself some coffee and sat down by the heater with Harry.

"Not flying?"

"Time off right now, cousin. Thought I'd hang around Kahiltna for a while."

"Slumming, huh?"

They laughed.

"Jets are nice," said Harry. It was a statement.

"Jets have their place," said the pilot.
"Do I detect a note of disillusionment?"
"Not really, no."
"Then why Kahiltna, Sam? With that airline pass of yours, you could go to Mexico City or Miami or someplace for practically nothing."
"I don't know…"
"I think I do," said Harry, standing and walking to the wall where some brown photographs were hanging.
"You come here because you belong here. You belong to this village and this village belongs to you."
"I don't live here anymore. I live in Anchorage."
"Nobody lives in Anchorage, Sam. Everybody stays in Anchorage, but nobody lives there. Nobody is from Anchorage, because that is not a place to be from. You know what I mean?"
"That's pretty far-fetched, Harry."
"Not really. Now, you take Kahiltna. Nobody knows for sure when man first settled here where the rivers come together. It is a natural den-up place for man. Here is his transportation, his timber, his water, his hunting grounds. This is a village where a person can be from. Where a person can live. Do you know how long your ancestors have lived here?"
"No."
"Neither do I, and no one else does either. But the white man has only been here for three generations. Our family can count back six, and that's only because we don't have records going back any farther."
"So, what are you getting at?"
"Just this. No matter if you are white man or Indian, or both, like you, this is a home village…an ancestral village. A person cannot leave it for long. The people here are your people, even though they are no blood relation. In the village, it is the village itself thst raises the children, disciplines them, rewards them for good deeds, approves of their marriages, rejoices in the births of their children and cries when they die. A village is a family, and you are a part of that family whether you like it or not. That's why you came back here on your time off. And that's why you'll keep coming back here every chance you get. And that's also why, deep in your mind, you plan to live here again. That house you dream about building will be here in this little jerkwater village."

Sam had been staring at the stove. Now he looked up at the dark piercing eyes of Harry Pete.
"How is it you know this?"
"Us full-blooded Indians know all kinds of stuff like that. You want I tell fortune by light of firestick?"

At the laughter, Mrs. Pete stuck her head out of the kitchen long enough to smile. At a look from her husband, she pulled it back in.

"Think about it, Sam," Harry said. "Think about it in all honesty, and you'll see I'm right."

"I'll think about it."

• • •

"How long has this been going on, Frank?" Buck asked, finishing his second beer in the South Seas.

"Almost ever since Pete died, and I'm getting tired of it."

The two men looked over at the round table, where Siwash Simmons had John Thompson cornered and was complaining bitterly.

"The more I think about," he said, "the more I think he did it on purpose. I mean, Kelly was kind of an ornery cuss, you see, and he used to do things like this to get under my skin."

"Siwash," Thompson said patiently, "surely a man can't help dying when it's his time."

"Well, a man has a right to die, that's true enough, but he doesn't have to take another man's new jacket with him, does he?" Siwash Simmons had forsworn beer and had been drinking his late partner's brand of medication ever since Pete Kelly died. He ordered another from Hemingway and brought it back to the table.

"I figure he did it on purpose, John," Siwash said. "He said himself he knew he was dying, didn't he?" He waved an arm around the near-empty barroom.

"Why, everybody in Kahiltna heard him say so, right here in this room! And that's why he did it. That's why he tricked me. 'Why not just let me borrow your brand-new forty-dollar jacket,' says he, and we'll trip the minuet around the street together…OLD PARTNER!" Simmons downed his drink and ordered another. From a sitting position this time.

Buck interrupted his speech. "You mean you think old Pete died with your jacket on just to get even, Simmons?"

"Indeed I do, in fact, indeed I certainly do. That ol' codger has been sore at me ever since the time I corrected his spelling on a note he left me. Can't help it if the man's uneducated. I was just trying to help."

"And you figure he died with your jacket on just to deprive you of it?"

"Can't think of why else he'd do it, Buck. Just mean, I guess. There just must've been a mean side to Pete Kelly that he'd kept hidden from us."

"For forty years?"

"See how sneaky he was?"

"Now wait a minute, Simmons. I got it all figured differently," Buck told him.

"How's that?"

"Well, you may not know this, but that night when we were all dancing, and he had your jacket?"

"Yeah?"

"Well, old Pete said to me, 'Buck, old fellow, you know I really think the world of that partner of mine.' And I agreed, you know, as I knew he really did. 'Yes' he says to me, 'and I sure hope nothing happens to this new jacket of Si's, because I know how much store he sets by it, and it cost him forty dollars and all.' Now does that sound sneaky to you, Siwash?"

"He really said that?"

"Sure he did. And so I got it figured differently than you do. I figured old Pete just lay down for a nap in your jacket, figurin' to give it back to you at breakfast, of course, and just died. Man can't help dyin', can he?"

"N-no, he can't."

"So I figure what old Pete would want is for us to go get your brand-new forty-dollar jacket back."

There were astonished looks around the barroom, but Siwash Simmons sat and scratched his beard and studied on it.

"Get it back, huh?"

"Why sure. Pete doesn't need it any more, and it'd be a shame to bury a brand-new forty-dollar jacket after breakup."

"Well, you know, that's right, now you mention it."

Hemingway and Frank each poured himself a drink , turning disbelieving faces toward one another as the conversation continued.

"Of course I'm right," Buck said. "So why don't we go over to the shed and get your jacket back. Your brand-new forty-dollar jacket."

"Great idea," Simmons said, staggering to his feet and slipping into his parka and mittens. "That Pete was a good ol' guy, all right. Wants to give me my jacket back…"

"That's right," Buck said, holding the door open for him, "and I've got a flashlight and two screwdrivers, so we're in business."

"Dang right!"

The two men shuffled off into the frozen night, leaving the remaining three men staring after them.

"I don't believe it," said Hemingway.

"Me neither," said John Thompson.

"I'll buy the drinks," said Frank, in a whisper. The others stared at him in surprise.

• • •

The flashlight swung around drunkenly inside the metal shed until it finally found the frosted snowmachine crate containing all that remained of Pete Kelly…and Siwash Simmons' new jacket. "Are you sure he won't mind, Buck?"

"Why are you whispering, Siwash?"

"It's just, well, you know…"

"Of course he won't mind," Buck said. "Now you get busy down at that end, and I'll unscrew these at this end, and before you know it, we'll have your jacket back."

"Right!"

Siwash's intentions were better than his aim with the screwdriver. When heavy arctic mittens are added to insobriety, the results can be less than dextrous. The screwdriver was slipping around the frosted surface of the casket lid in desperate search of a screw. Buck noticed the problem.

"Look, old-timer, you just hold the light and I'll unscrew the lid."

"Right."

"Hold it still, now."

"R-r-right!"

"That's better," Buck said, getting one screw out. "A few more screws and we'll be ready for the ax…"

"Ax? The ax?"

Buck looked up briefly at Siwash, then returned to his work.

"Sure we're gonna need an ax," Buck said, matter-of-factly, "to get the arms broken, you know."

"Arms broken!"

"Why hell yes, Simmons. Old Pete's been dead four days out here and it's been twenty below. We'll have to break both his arms to get your jacket off him. He'll be stiffer'n a brick."

"Break his arms?"

"Sure. Both of them," Buck said, still unscrewing the lid. "Of course, Old Pete won't feel a thing, being dead and all, so it won't matter a damn if we break his arms. And I know he'd want you to have your brand-new forty-dollar jacket back."

"Buck, wait. We can't break his arms!"

Davis stopped his work and thought a minute, then smiled and went to work again.

"You're absolutely right, Simmons. Too much chance of hurting that jacket. Of course, it'll be much easier and safer the other way."

"What other way, Buck?"

"Why, we'll just cut his arms off at the shoulder, then we'll slip each arm out of the sleeves, and we'll have your jacket back with no damage to it.

Brilliant idea, Siwash. Glad you thought of it."

"Cut his arms off!"

"Sure. Faster, too. Then you can have your brand-new forty-dollar jacket back even quicker. And old Pete will rest easy, knowing that his beloved old partner got his brand-new forty-dollar jacket back."

"Buck, wait!" Siwash grabbed Buck's arm.

"Wait now, Buck, I just got an idear. Now just think about this, OK? OK. Now old Pete and I was partners, you know, and I loved him like a brother. Well, you know what I'm going to do, Buck?"

"What's that, Siwash?"

The old trapper was seen to smile in the dimming glow of the flashlight.

"Why, I'm going to give my partner that brand-new forty-dollar jacket for a funeral present!"

"Well you know, Siwash," Buck said thoughtfully, "that's a mighty generous thing you just did. It is for sure."

Then Buck Davis smiled to himself and replaced the screws in the frost-whitened snowmachine crate.

chapter 14

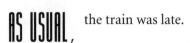

AS USUAL, the train was late.

Lester Douglas sat by the window as the endless forest rolled by, glancing at his watch impatiently from time to time. His young wife, Sherry, sat quietly, watching the forest slide past and finding there some private pleasures that brought smiles to her face.

"According to this schedule, we should've been there ten minutes ago," Douglas said.

"We'll get there, Les."

He looked down at his wife.

"You don't really care much if we get out to your uncle's cabin today or not, do you?"

"It's been there a long time, you know," she replied. "It can wait for a while longer. What's your hurry, Les? We've got all the rest of our lives to live there."

"Women…"

Douglas fingered the empty holster on his hip, and the missing hardware there made him even more irritable. Sherry had been embarrassed by the scene he had caused when the conductor asked him to leave the big revolver in his pack until he got off the train.

The usual crowd was waiting for the Tuesday train in Kahiltna. Additions to the regulars were Siwash Simmons and Buck Davis, who stood by Buck's car as the train braked to a stop. The willing hands of passengers and onlookers alike helped hand down the mail sacks, then the luggage, then finally load on the luggage of passengers getting on for the ride north to Fairbanks.

"How will we know which ones they are?" Simmons asked Buck.

"Can't be too many passengers. We'll find them."

The question was answered sooner than they expected. A booming voice yelled, "Who the hell is Davis?"

The men looked up to see a huge figure of a man dressed in buckskins, with a gunfighter's tied-down quick-draw rig strapped to his belt.

"You suppose that's him?" Simmons asked.

"Wouldn't be surprised," Buck said, walking over to the man.

"I'm Buck Davis," he said, holding out his hand.

"Right, right," Douglas said, shaking it quickly and then looking for his luggage. "Let's get this stuff loaded as quickly as we can and get going. This damn train was almost fifteen minutes late."

"Always is," said Siwash. "Where's your missus?"

"Are you Mr. Simmons?" Sherry asked.

"No, I'm not, honey," he said, throwing his arms around her. "I'm Siwash Simmons, or Uncle Siwash, or something like that, anyway. I was your uncle Pete's partner, and I'll be your closest neighbor, too."

"I'm so glad to meet you," Sherry said, smiling.

Douglas stopped looking for his gun and cleared his throat.

"This might be a good time to get a few things clear," he said. "Whatever business arrangements you might have had with Sherry's uncle don't apply to me. I'm a loner, and I plan to stay a loner. I don't need help, and I don't need advice, and we'll get along fine if you just stay on your trap line and I stay on mine."

Siwash looked at Buck with a quizzical expression.

"Pete Kelly and I was partners, which is to say, well, I mean…"

"What he's trying to say, Douglas," Buck said, "is that being partners had nothing to do with business. It just had to do with being partners."

"That's right," Siwash nodded. "Thanks, Buck."

"I take it you folks want to fly in this afternoon?" Buck asked.

"Of course. There's no sense in waiting around here, is there? Might as well get started."

"Les, couldn't we just stay overnight and get acquainted? It won't matter if we wait just one more day."

"And do what? Spend money here, I suppose. No. We'll leave today. That is, if Mr. Davis here approves."

"OK by me," Davis said, "and everybody calls me Buck."

"Then let's go."

Simmons gave Sherry another hug and whispered that he would be over from time to time to see how they were doing. She smiled at him in thanks.

Siwash walked sadly back to the South Seas Roadhouse while Douglas and Buck loaded the gear.

"You kids have everything you need?" Buck asked.

"Yes, we have," Douglas answered. "Bought it in Seattle before we came up. We knew what prices were going to be up here."

Buck shrugged his shoulders in resignation and drove to the airstrip. Douglas managed to find his pistol and returned it to the low-slung holster. He stared defiantly straight ahead as they drove past the South Seas.

Siwash and John Thompson stuck their heads out the door of the roadhouse and watched as the car went by on its way to the airplane.

"A gunfighter rig?"

"That's right, John, a gunfighter rig."

"What about the girl?"

"She's sweet as pie."

"Well," Thompson said, raising his bottle of Oly in a prophetic salute, "here's to the innocent pilgrims of this world. May they survive."

"May they survive," whispered Siwash Simmons.

chapter 15

TRAPPER SWENSON'S CABIN was under a deep layer of snow and disuse when Hemingway Jones arrived in the orange twilight of a wintry afternoon.

Using a snowshoe as a shovel, he first cleared the doorway, unloaded the toboggan and put his gear inside. Then, remembering the advice of the experienced sourdoughs, he banged on the stovepipes to clear obstructions, then shoveled snow from around the cap on the pipe. More than one bush resident had suffocated because of neglecting this chore.

Obviously Swenson had been a conscientious cabin dweller, if an eccentric one, for Hemingway found an ample supply of firewood under the adjoining lean-to. The ten years since Swenson's departure had allowed the wood to season nicely, and in no time fire roared in both the heater and the cookstove. It was still too cold to sit down, so Hemingway spent the next hour with a broom and shovel, making the tiny place livable. By the time the frost had receded to the plywood floor, Hemingway had removed his outer clothes and had a large pan of snow melting for coffee.

Taking stock of the log home, he saw no immediate indication of the old Swede's eccentricity. Hemingway didn't know exactly what to expect, of course, but the tiny cabin of a man whose lifelong hatred of aircraft had become a statewide legend should have reflected this, he thought.

Many people thought Swenson should have been removed years earlier, of course, but if he had been, a lot would have been missing from Alaskana.

It began shortly after the old trapper had built the cabin. By some vagary of fate, the cabin lay in a direct line from the end of the village airstrip. Most aircraft leaving for the north passed over his cabin. This bothered the old Swede more than most people realized until several years had passed.

On one of Swenson's rare trips to the village, he had taken a large envelope with him to the small railroad depot and bought a ticket for Anchorage. The following day, he went to the local newspaper office with his envelope and walked up to the advertising desk.

"I vant to put dis in de paper," he told the girl.

The girl looked at the carefully printed page from the envelope. "Is this a joke, sir?"

"No joke. I vant put dis in de paper. I pay."

"I think it's against the law, sir."

The old trapper became annoyed.

"Vat happen to freedom of de press? I vant put dis in de paper."

"Just a minute, please."

She returned with the manager, and after a few minutes of conversation with the adamant old trapper, it was decided that the old man's advertisement would run, with a disclaimer alongside from the paper itself. This was fine with Swenson.

The following day, and for a week after, people were talking about the ad:

> WARNING TO PILOTS Do not fly over my cabin on Kahiltna River making noise and scaring dogs. If you do this, I will have to shoot your machine. Fly somewhere else. Alaska is big, you don't have to fly over my house.
>
> Signed, Olaf Swenson
> Kahiltna River near the bluffs

When he rode the train back to Kahiltna, he stopped in at the South Seas Roadhouse for a whiskey. Frank Granger remarked that the advertisement was a good gag, and everyone had got a good chuckle out of it.

"No gag, Frank," Swenson said solemnly. "I mean effery vord."

"But why, Swenson? Surely you don't mean you'll shoot at an airplane?"

"Don't vant to," he said, "but I vill. I hate 'em."

Swenson walked out of the roadhouse and on up the river to begin the legend.

Several days later, the first pilot reported he had been shot at by some old codger at a cabin to the north of the village. Buck Davis flew up to see whether this was correct, and immediately wheeled and headed back for the village when Swenson ran from the cabin brandishing a .303 Enfield. Troopers were sent out to warn Swenson against shooting at any aircraft in the neighborhood, and they were received warmly by the old trapper. After all, he told them, he didn't hate visitors, just airplanes.

The troopers returned to the village shaking their heads and saying they didn't know what they could do at this point, since Swenson had never actually hit anyone yet, but they suggested to the local pilots that they avoid Swenson's airspace until something could be figured out to end this situation.

As it turned out, the situation continued for a number of years. Once in a great while some Anchorage pilot would report being shot at while flying over the cabin, and the flight service stations in the basin marked out a small square on the big maps that was simply called "hazardous area." The pilots referred to Swenson's airspace as "Flak City."

Swenson's hatred of aircraft came to be the subject of jokes and stories, and added to the color of the village. Pilots avoided the cabin on their flights, and life seemed destined to continue without incident until Swenson killed the helicopter.

During one extremely hot July, a fire began over on the east side of the hills and was driven west by higher and higher winds. The only habitation directly in the path of the blaze was Swenson's cabin, and some well-meaning fire fighters flew in to evacuate him and his dogs in a large government helicopter.

Swenson stepped out the door of the cabin with the Enfield and waited until the helicopter was firmly on the ground and the occupants were away from it. Then he put a 215-grain solid bullet through the engine.

At the trial, the prosecution had a rough time of it. Consider, Swenson's lawyer said, the facts: 1. Ample warning was given in a large newspaper, 2. No one was injured, 3. The helicopter was trespassing on private property, and 4. The wind changed direction and the fire didn't even get close to the cabin.

The trial had excited a lot of interest, and the nervous judge was afraid he would have to make a very unpopular decision, when the day was saved by someone from the prosecutor's office. During routine research, it was learned that Swenson had been in Alaska illegally for more than forty years. The charges were dropped, and trapper Swenson disappeared into legend with a one-way ticket back to Sweden.

Hemingway chuckled at the memory and made some coffee. With dinner cooking, the cabin clean and the atmosphere warm and cheery, Hemingway Jones was aware of the silence. When a man in a remote cabin sits quietly, there is nothing but the low rumbling of wood burning in the heater and the occasional drip of melting snow off the eaves. There was in Hemingway Jones a driving urge to write. Well, perhaps not to write, but to be a writer. He knew inside that he was able to sit back and see things in life that others often missed. The painful part came when he sat down with paper and pen and faced the blank page. The lofty, wonderful, poetic thoughts and descriptions that occurred to him in the quiet moments evaded him when faced with the paper. It was seldom that he got past the first word.

He got out the paper and pen and sat there in the low, comfortable light of the kerosene lamp and nothing happened. Perhaps, he thought, tonight would be a good time to plan what to write, and then morning would be a good time to actually write it. He could outline what he was going to write on the paper tonight, so it would be fresh in the morning.

After all, he reasoned, he was tired from the long walk. The snowshoes had given his unaccustomed muscles a dose of *mal de racquet,* the "snowshoe sickness" of the voyageurs, and he knew tomorrow would be agony. The hearty meal he ate was twice as much as he normally ate for dinner, and he was feeling better than he had in years.

He would sit and think and let the stories come, tonight. When they came, he would jot down the ideas and let tomorrow be a fresh day for writing.

Hemingway loaded the stove full for the night, shutting the draft and dampering it full. Stretching out full in Frank's sleeping bag on the cot, he thought for a minute, then wrote "Buck's wolverines" on the paper and blew out the lamp.

Buck Davis had been telling Hemingway one night a matter-of-fact story of how to catch wolverines without damaging their valuable pelts. Completely beyond credulity, Hemingway listened without interrupting.

"Course, this was long ago, Hem," Buck had said, sipping a cold one. "Couldn't do it now. Need to be fast."

"The trick to catching a wolverine is to wait until the snow conditions are just right. Deep powder snow just after a fresh snowfall is ideal. In fact, that's the only time you can catch one. When the snow gets a crust after a hard freeze, those wolverines can just hump along like ninety.

"What I'd do is just fly around until I saw one hopping along that funny way they have in deep snow. Then I'd land the aircraft, strap on some snowshoes and go after him. It'd take some good shuffling to catch up with one, but after about a quarter of a mile, I'd come on him. That's the tricky part, right there.

"You see, Hemingway, any wild animal will fight when cornered, and a wolverine will fight any time at all. So when you corner a wolverine, you definitely have your hands full.

"So now comes the tricky part. You gotta time this just right, see. When you get about six feet from him, a wolverine will turn at bay and attack. When that happens, you lift one snowshoe to give him a target. He jumps for that shoe, and then you step forward with it and push him down into the snow. Now, a wolverine hates to have anyone stand on him, even in soft snow, so he'll tunnel around with his head down to crawl out and get you. And that's when you get him."

"That's when you get him?" Hemingway asked.

"Right. When he has his head down, the back of his neck is unprotected, and his claws are beneath him, floundering around in that deep snow. When he does this, you just reach down with your hand, grab him by the back of the neck, and shove him face down into the snow until he suffocates."

Hemingway began laughing, and he laughed louder and louder the more he thought of it. It was as funny as the would-be hunting expert who suggested spitting into the mouth of an African lion, should you be attacked.

Buck looked a little hurt. "Well, go ahead and laugh. I didn't say I could still do it. But that's how it was done back a few years ago."

Buck put a dollar on the bar and stood up to leave.

"No, no, Buck." Hemingway laughed as he handed the dollar back. "This one's on me. That's the best story I've heard in a month!"

Buck simply shrugged and left the bar.

Hemingway looked toward Frank, who was sitting in his corner with yesterday's Anchorage paper, and Harry Pete, who nursed his coffee at the jukebox end of the bar.

"It finally happened!" Hemingway almost shouted for joy. "I finally caught Buck Davis in a windy! Smothering wolverines with his bare hands.!"

"Seen him do it once," said Frank, turning back to his paper.

"Me too," Harry Pete put in. "Use to fly spotter for him. I've seen him kill them that way twice. Show you the pictures someday."

"Oh, come on! You guys are kidding me!"

"Nope," said Frank. "I've known Buck Davis since he first came into this country. Never once knew him to tell a windy."

"Hey, Hemingway," Harry said. "Buck ever tell you the time he pulled the tail off a live coyote?"

"No."

"Ask him about it sometime. I hear it was pretty funny. My brother was with him when it happened."

With the memory of that story on his mind, Hemingway Jones reveled in the warmth of the sleeping bag, the chuckling of the stove, and the silent secrets of the black frozen world outside the cabin. He smiled and went to sleep.

Four days later, Hemingway Jones snowshoed back across the river and into the village. After greeting the regulars in the roadhouse, he went upstairs and returned Frank's gear. Frank was sitting at his usual table reading yesterday's Anchorage paper. He put it down as Hemingway brought a cup of coffee over to the table and sat down.

"How was the trip?"

"I don't know, Frank. Oh, hell, I didn't get anything written at all. Took a few notes, that's all."

"Cabin need a lot of fixing?"

"No. It was fine. Lots of firewood."

Frank took off his glasses and spoke in a low friendly voice.

"Let me guess what happened, son. You'd wake up in the morning and get a morning fire and breakfast. Then you'd have a cup of coffee and think about the strange country you were in, and you'd put on your snowshoes and go exploring."

"Yes."

"Then you found yourself being monopolized by the country. You'd spend more and more time each day looking at animal tracks in the snow and wondering what they were. You'd walk and look at the chickadees and the ravens and hope you'd see a moose or two."

"Saw a cow and a calf yesterday."

"That's what I mean. Then you'd find yourself thinking in different types of time. Things you wanted to do one afternoon, you found easy to put off until tomorrow. And you got to liking the cabin, and your sense of self-reliance, and you began thinking more and more of spending a good deal of time out at that cabin. And you started doing little things around the cabin to make it more livable. Right?"

"I put together some bookshelves."

"Did you take any books with you?"

"Well, no, now that you mention it."

"And you didn't even realize it, did you? That means you're planning to go back. And that's a good thing, Hemingway."

"But I didn't get any writing done, Frank.", I

"So you're feeling guilty about it, right? Well, son, I watched you walk up the street and never saw you walk so straight before. That tanned face of yours would mark you as a bush rat anyway, and I bet you've gained a few pounds of muscle. That's in just, what, four days? Think of what a week would do, or a month, or a season. And what you've done is absolutely essential to being a writer."

"But I didn't write, Frank."

"Yes, but you lived. Now you know why people choose to live out here. Sure, you could write the stories people tell when they come in here, but your stories wouldn't have any understanding in them. Did you remember to put the morning kindling in the oven to dry overnight?"

"Yes. Just like you said."

"And it worked, and you'll never forget it, will you? You'll remember that lesson all your life, and it will be in your stories, and folks will know that you've been there and know what you're talking about. Now what you do is to listen more and more, and make notes more and more, and live out in the Bush more and more. Someday the writing will come to you. The story will be there, and you'll be ready to write it. Your story isn't ready yet, son. When it is, it'll tell you, and you'll be able to write it, and write it well."

Hemingway Jones smiled. "Maybe you're right, Frank."

"You bet I'm right, kid."

Frank picked up his glasses and his paper, then took one more look at Hemingway.

"There's dirty dishes in the kitchen. We saved 'em for you."

chapter 16

"SIWASH SIMMONS is the race marshal!" Frank Granger yelled to the crowd.

"He will see to it that no cheating takes place!"

Frank paused, out of breath, and admitted it was hard work yelling to be heard over the frantic barking and screaming of Harry Pete's dogs.

Harry and Sam Davis were harnessing dogs and leading them up to the long gang line. Harry's leader, Crabmeat, lunged silently against the tugline, eager to be going. He held his head at an angle, because of the blind eye. From time to time he turned and growled at the lunging swing dogs behind him.

Harry's team was securely tied to the bumper of a pickup truck, which rocked with each lunge the team made.

On the other side of Frank Granger was John Thompson, who was making last-minute checks of his snowmachine. He smiled and gunned the engine from time to time. Both contestants were finally ready and were brought together to shake hands. It was a mock-solemn occasion, marked by Frank Granger's wearing of a dark pin-striped suit, bedecked by a gold watch that hadn't seen daylight since the Chicago fire.

"This is the race," Frank intoned, "that will settle once and for all the long-standing dispute about which is best for cross-country travel, a dog team or a snow-go.

"The racers will go through the swamps and the timber to the old Benson cabin, go around behind the cabin, and come back to town. All the proprieties will be observed scrupulously. There will be no cheating by either of you, not even you, John Thompson. And the race marshal is reminded at this time that sobriety is a must when judging a contest of this magnitude."

He motioned to both contestants and Simmons to come closer.

"The winner of this race will be determined by which of you comes through the door of the South Seas first, is that understood? Good. Hemingway will cook a steak dinner for the winner, which will be paid for, in cash, by the loser. Is that clear? Good."

Frank cleared his throat, stuck his thumbs into his vest pockets, and yelled to the assembled host.

"Gentlemen, start your engine and your mutts!"

Both men walked to their vehicles, while an attendant carefully slipped mittens on them and put the connecting "idiot string" over their parka hoods to prevent mitten loss.

John revved his engine and pulled down his goggles. Harry checked the ties on his mukluks, then reached behind him for the slipknot that would release his straining team from the truck.

When all was ready, Siwash Simmons pulled an old Webley .45 revolver from his belt and held it in the air. When all of Harry's dogs were facing forward, there was an ear-splitting roar from the gun, and the race was on.

Buck Davis, gently circling the village in the Super Cub, was really the only person who watched the entire race besides the contestants. He banked the plane and saw John Thompson's snowmachine take a quick lead down the snow-covered dirt road toward the forest, the dog team close behind.

Crabmeat's one good eye was focused on the disappearing rooster tail of snow behind Thompson's snowmachine, and the old dog poured all he had into the contest. His teammates were in a flat-out sprint behind him as they silently charged down the trail after the noisy machine.

Buck smiled slyly when he saw Thompson's snowmachine leave the road to cut through a broad band of spruce along side. The machine took the turn too quickly, and spun out into a drift. While Thompson wrestled the machine, the dog team streaked past him, with hoots from Harry Pete as they passed.

The dogs held the lead through the twistings and turnings of the forest trail, and through the broad dip of Question Creek. As the sled crossed the ice of the creek, Harry felt a flexing in the ice. He looked back in alarm as they shot across and up the far bank. The surface wasn't bad, but there was a give to it. What would happen when the heavier snowmachine crossed? He didn't wait around to learn, but pumped hard with his right foot as his team lined out perfectly and streaked onto the giant muskeg swamp system.

Seconds later, John Thompson's snowmachine barreled across Question Creek and roared faster and faster across the frozen swamp after the dog team. Behind him, but unnoticed by the driver, there were trickles of water oozing into the tread tracks going across the heaving ice of the creek.

In the open swamp, a 25-mph dog team stands no chance against a 60-mph snowmachine, and John Thompson was quick to take advantage of this. Swinging off the trail, he blazed through the field of snow with the throttle wide open, passing to the left of the dog team. His cheers and taunts could be heard even above the roar of the engine, as he passed the dog team and regained the lead.

Harry Pete did not let up on his pumping, nor on encouraging his team. Crabmeat's good eye again focused on the roaring machine that threatened to make him obsolete, and poured more determination into his running. The fits and starts of a team starting out had now been smoothed until, from the air, Harry Pete's dog team was a syncopated ballet of silent speed, winding through the turns of the swamp like a snake in pursuit of a noisy fleeing mouse.

Buck also saw that the roaring mouse was headed for a narrow strip of trees at a tremendous rate of speed. If the trail went straight through, he thought, John shouldn't have any trouble. But if there were any curves…

There were no curves, but there was something else.

For a reason known only to Nature, the heavy snows of winter occasionally bend the pliant birches and alders to the ground, piling even more snow on them, and stringing them taut and quivering like a hunting bow.

John's snowmachine was heading directly for a tall birch in this arched position. It wasn't until just before he passed beneath the arch that he noticed the short branch sticking down.

He didn't have time to yell before the branch caught beneath his parka hood. The snowmachine continued another eighty feet without John, then died in a snowbank. Thompson didn't pay much attention, though, as he was becoming part of the tree. His weight had struck the branch at close to 50 mph, and physics had quickly computed the mass and speed and foot pounds of energy, and decided John Thompson was enough to free the top of the tree from the snow.

As Crabmeat ran, he saw the skeletal form of the tree rise straight up in front of him, with what appeared to be a wildly kicking scarecrow suspended by his parka hood from an upper branch.

Harry Pete snatched the snow hook from the sled and jammed it into the snow, dragging it until it finally caught and stopped his team. He stepped off the sled and looked casually up at the tree.

"You know, Crabmeat," he said, "a man can find the strangest things hanging around in the woods."

"Harry, you just gotta get me down!" pleaded John.

"Did you hear something, C.M.? No? Well, I guess it was just the wind, after all. Man's mind plays funny tricks on him in the woods, don't it?"

"OK. OK, Harry, you had a good laugh. Now look, I can't get hold of anything up here, and I reckon I'll just stay here and rot if you don't do something."

"Now Crabmeat," Harry said softly, "just what kind of an animal do you think we have here in our snare?"

Crabmeat looked up at the swaying figure with his good eye.

"Now, I don't figure anything that mean can be much good on the fur market, do you?"

"OK Harry. Ha ha HA! Now would you get me down from here!"

"Makes a lot of noise, too, Crab. Now, normally I wouldn't want anything that smelled that bad or made that much noise, but we could always use some firewood. What do you say?"

"Firewood? Harry Pete, what we need now is to get me down out of this tree!"

"There's that noise again, Crabmeat."

"OK, OK, please get me down out of this tree, Harry."

"Why sure, John, old buddy. You just wait right there while I get the ax."

"Of course I'll wait right here. Where else am I? The ax? Did you say ax??"

"Yep. Always carry one in the sled. Plumb forgot to bring the ladder, John, so I guess this ax will have to do."

"Harry, it's a half-mile from here to the ground. Just what are you…"

"John, I'm going to chop down the tree. Here's the ax, and I'm about ready…"

"You crazy Indian! You mean you're going to cut down this…!"

"Crab, you hear that animal screaming again? Yeah, me too. Oh well, nothing like cutting a little firewood to help keep a man warm."

Harry Pete took long, measured strokes on the birch's trunk. Each blow sent quivers up the tree, and set its unwilling tenant jerking like a puppet on a string.

"Harry! For the love of Mike!"

"Crabmeat, did you know that firewood warms you twice? That's right. It warms you when you cut it, and warms you again when you burn it."

Crabmeat rested with his head on his paws and looked up at John Thompson, swinging in the breeze.

"Harry, what have I ever done to you?"

"Now just listen to that, Crab. Here I am, taking time away from winning this race to come to the aid of my fellow human being, and what thanks do I get?"

"But Harry, the ax…!!"

"You see, Crabmeat, I figure I got two alternatives. I can either cut down this tree and rescue my fellow racer, which means, of course, that I stand a chance of losing the race to him, or I could just go ahead, win the race, and after I've eaten my steak dinner at the South Seas, I could send someone back out here for Mr. Thompson so he can pay the bill. Now that I think about it, maybe it would be better to leave him here."

"OK, OK, Harry. You win. But can you cut the tree down gently?"

"We're about to find out, John."

There was a loud pop, then some cracking, and Harry had thrown the ax back into the sled and pulled the hook before the tree was halfway to the ground. His dogs were in a full run before the screaming John Thompson became part of a deep snowbank.

By the time Thompson started his machine and straightened it out, the dog team had nearly a half-mile lead on him, and he drove across the swamp system wide open to make up the difference.

Swamp systems are home to many creatures, and this day one of the largest was at home, nibbling at some snow-covered willows just off the race trail. The cow moose looked up, saw the approaching dog team, and trotted away across the swamp.

Somewhere in Alaska there may dwell a dog that can take a moose or leave it alone. Maybe. But there is something about the high-kneed trot of a moose, coupled with the haughty carriage of its head and the taunting of its stupid facial expression, that brings out the carnivore in a dog. Especially a sled dog.

In a team of dogs, the effect of sighting a moose is multiplied by the number of dogs, and then a sense of lynch-mob hysteria takes over. When that particular team is led by a one-eyed curmudgeon named Crabmeat, who lost an eye to a moose in puppyhood, the effect is disastrous.

The team increased its speed almost ten miles an hour, running on adrenaline and whining with anticipation. It left the trail and headed straight across the swamp toward the moose.

Harry was doing his best to stop the team. He stood on the spring brake with both feet and dragged the hook with his right hand, but the soft snow of the swamp was not a retardant to hooks and brakes. It was as useless as trying to stop a train by dragging a foot.

The moose increased her speed, but the team was gaining. It would be only moments now before the moose would turn at bay and begin carving dogs and musher to rags with her front feet.

Harry Pete caught a blur out of the corner of his vision, and thought he heard a roar, and then looked with amazement as John Thompson left his machine in a wide dive and bulldogged Crabmeat.

With the leader firmly implanted under John's arm, the dogs swung in an arc until they were a growling, yapping tangle of harnesses, lines, and fur.

With both men dug in, holding down the lead and swing dogs, the team came to a halt, and the moose escaped into the timber. With the moose gone, the dogs lined out perfectly and began a good, controlled run once more toward Benson's cabin and the turnaround point. The team again shot into the lead while Thompson sprinted for his snowmachine.

Gaining ground on the dog team, John Thompson saw that Harry and the dogs would reach the halfway point before he did. Just as the team disappeared from sight around the cabin, John reached into a saddlebag, pulled out a dried salmon, kissed it, and dropped it in the trail with a wicked grin.

The team rounded the cabin and started back down the trail as John and his machine started around the other side of the empty house. Harry waved and grinned in triumph as they passed, but John just chuckled as he disappeared behind the cabin.

It happened in the blink of an eye.

Crabmeat had been cruising along at a good, happy run when he spotted something ahead in the trail that didn't belong. It was coming up fast, and it was hard to tell, but it sorta resembled, yes, a little, but with one eye it was hard to tell, but then again, you know, it even smells a bit like, it's passing beneath my front—

FISH! FISH! FISH!

Crabmeat dived for it, but turned a complete somersault. The swing dogs made a grab for it, but were going just a bit too fast and tripped over Crabmeat as he tunneled back through the team like a mole with a goal.

The first set of team dogs had slowed down enough to grab the fish. One had the head, the other had the tail. Then Crabmeat had the head of one dog and another had his tail.

All this happened at 20 mph. Harry didn't even have time for a quick prayer before the sled slammed into the growing mountain of dogs and stopped.

Just like that. Stopped.

Harry did a flip over the driving bow, rolled across the sled basket, and dived into the team. Somehow he escaped being bitten.

He crawled out of the teeth and fur and was grabbing for a dog's tail when John Thompson passed him, waving and singing, "It was sad when the great ship went down..."

By the time Harry wrestled the fish away from the dogs, chopped it into pieces with his knife, and distributed them fairly among the dogs, Thompson had an unbeatable lead.

Harry Pete knew a race wasn't over until it ended, however, so he quickly started his team back down the trail. Crabmeat proudly held a piece of salmon in his mouth as he streaked back toward home.

Increasing his lead, John Thompson knew he had the race won when he was only halfway across the big swamp. He looked behind him, but saw no sign of the dog team.

John's singing slowed down, and then stopped. Then the machine stopped as John twisted around to look behind him for the team. It wasn't in sight.

Maybe Harry was bitten in the fight. Maybe some of the dogs were hurt. What did I do now? I didn't mean any real harm. Just a little fish in the trail. Old Indian trick, right? Lots of fun. But what if Harry's hurt?

John was just about to turn around and check on the dog team when Crabmeat burst into sight, leading the charging horde of fishburners, his chunk of salmon clearly visible.

"Hit it! Hit it!" yelled Harry. "Hike, you mangy garbage grinders!"

The dogs responded with a fresh burst of speed.

All right, John grinned. All right!

His machine roared into action again and was soon up to speed, scooting across the swamp. Crabmeat and company had dropped back a little as Thompson increased his lead. He knew now he had to make as much time as he could here on the flats, because the dogs could maneuver through the approaching timber much faster than he could. He planned to maintain top speed until just after he crossed Question Creek, then throttle back for the wiggle through the trees, followed by a quick dash down the road to the finish line.

It wasn't to be.

Buck Davis was the only one who really saw what happened. He had begun laughing even before the snowmachine reached Question Creek. From the air he saw the spreading dark stain around the ice at the creek crossing. He saw the stain grow, saw the water get deeper. He knew what was about to happen, and could do nothing about it but watch and laugh and maintain airspeed.

He didn't hear the singing, though, as John Thompson poured on the gas, heading for the creek.

"Husbands and wives…little biddy children lost their lives…it was sad when the grea-a-at ship went…"

The snowmachine hit the open water at 63 mph.

"…*down!*"

The resultant rooster tail of water drenched spruce trees for twenty yards in each direction.

• • •

Frank Granger looked at his gold watch as he paced. Hemingway paced behind him. Siwash Simmons was taking some medication outside the door to the South Seas Roadhouse.

"They should've been back in by now," Frank said.

"Maybe they had an accident," said Hemingway.

Frank looked significantly at Siwash.

"What you mean," said Siwash, "is that maybe they had an 'on purpose.'"

One of the kids down the road yelled, "Here they come!"

The half-empty street immediately filled with people. Binoculars were produced. Siwash snatched a pair away from a neighbor and focused.

"It's Crabmeat!"

The villagers could see Crabmeat and the team coming down the road at a stately trot. They saw something else, too. From a comfortable position in the sled, waving to the crowd, was John Thompson. Trailing along behind Harry Pete as he pumped to help the dogs was Thompson's snowmachine, being towed ignominiously home by the conquering dog team.

From his seat in the sled, John Thompson turned his head to look back at Harry.

"You know, Harry, it's really decent of you to tow me in like this."

"That's OK, John, I want you to be around to pay for my steak."

John had been toying with a dog snap that was used to keep a dog in the sled if it was being hauled for some reason. The idea didn't come at once. It filtered in as the sled, with its heavy load of soggy snowmachine, approached the village and the crowd outside the roadhouse.

John looked back at Harry over his shoulder. Harry was pumping and urging the dogs along, waving joyfully from time to time at the crowd.

"Isn't that Siwash there by the door?" John asked.

Harry focused his attention on the faraway door of the South Seas. As he looked, he failed to see John Thompson silently attach the dog snap to the idiot string connecting Harry's mittens.

"It was a fine race, Harry."

"That it was, John. And that steak is going to taste mighty good, too."

"Oh yeah, about that steak. I hope you have enough money to pay for it, Harry."

"Me? The steak's on you, John, I mean…"

"Correct me if I'm wrong, sir. Did not our illustrious race judge say that the winner would be the first one through the door of the South Seas?"

"Yes." An uneasy thought passed through Harry's mind.

"Tally ho!" shouted John, jumping from the sled and sprinting the final hundred yards to the South Seas.

"Why, you…!"

Harry left the sled and ran after him, but the line came taut on his mittens, and he was jerked down like a tarpon and dragged along behind the sled, kicking and squirming.

The crowd roared as John Thompson ran the final few feet to the door of the South Seas. Holding his hands in the air in a victory salute, he prepared to step across the threshold.

"This is one small step for man," he declared, "and a giant leap for snowmachines."

He didn't hear the warning shout as he was about to take the step, and so didn't see Crabmeat dive between his legs and charge into the South Seas. All he knew was that he was suddenly in a sea of fur, chairs, and tuglines, swimming to regain his feet.

"One juicy sirloin steak, rare, with potatoes and gravy and vegetables. Hope he likes vegetables."

Hemingway emerged from the kitchen with the steaming steak.

"It's not fair," grumbled John Thompson from his bar stool.

"A waste of a good meal," growled Harry Pete.

"Gentlemen," announced Siwash Simmons, "you were both informed of the race rules. They were clear-cut and in plain English. Also, the race marshal's decision is final, and that's all there is to it. Hemingway, you may serve the winning meal, if you will."

"My pleasure, entirely," grinned Hemingway, and he placed the steak dinner under Crabmeat's nose. All in the room cheered. The one-eyed lead dog ate the vegetables last.

chapter 17

LES DOUGLAS wasn't sure what there was about cutting firewood that galled him so.

Had he been one to analyze situations, he would probably have discovered it was the urgency and the steady pressure of supplying firewood that caused his disgust, his irritation. A man with a sense of humor in the Bush finds in cutting firewood a good source for laughter. Had Douglas been one of these, there would have been less of a problem.

One young bush dweller with a mathematical bent sat down one day and covered several sheets of paper with figures. He didn't tell his wife what the project was until the next time they took the train to town.

She noticed he stepped onto the train in an unusually jaunty manner, and began visiting with some elderly tourists. One retired executive took a look at the rough clothing and beard of the mountain man and asked the inevitable question.

"Young man, just what is it you do for a living?"

Beaming with pleasure, he took a small card from his pocket, looked closely at the figures there, and announced, "Last year I cut down 67 trees, made more than 2,000 saw cuts, carried eight tons of wood a distance of 900 miles, and swung a nine-pound splitting maul more than 10,952 times. How about you, Pop?"

But Les Douglas was not blessed with a sense of humor. To him, there was nothing humorous about the Woodpile Problem. He resented its constant demands. Perhaps it would be easier to take, had he been more successful in other areas of woods life. If, for example, he had been receptive to advice from experienced residents, he might have been more successful as a trapper. But he had put all his traps within a half-mile of the cabin on Lynx Lake, had refused to take certain precautions in the handling and placement of the traps, and consequently had caught only a curious raven to date. In a rage, the would-be trapper had beaten the glossy bird to death with a rifle stock.

The cold weather hadn't helped any, he thought. A man couldn't be expected to cut wood or run a trap line in subzero weather. And when it did warm up enough, it snowed. When he cut down a tree during or right after a snow, every swing of the ax brought a shower of powder snow out of the branches and down the back of his neck. And then, if he waited to buck the tree up into firewood and haul it in, a fresh snowfall covered it, making it nearly impossible to find before spring.

And the fresh snow covered the traps, rendering them useless. He had already misplaced a dozen and wouldn't find them before breakup. They all had to be dug up and reset after each snowfall. And just when that happened, it seemed, the bottom would fall out of the thermometer and Sherry would be burning more firewood.

She burned it constantly.

And when it was really cold, I mean really cold, she kept the cook stove burning as well as the sheet-metal heater. Since the cook stove took only small pieces of wood, the larger chunks cut for the heater had to be split even further.

And the darkness. There were only about four hours of daylight each day now. Four hours. There wasn't enough daylight to accomplish all that needed to be done.

Hauling the water. Two buckets every day. And she wanted more. Firewood. Trapping. And then it was dark before a man even gets to the firewood. And she says she works hard in the house. It's warm in the house. It's light in the house. And there's this little crawling...

Fear. This little crawling fear.

No, just a little doubt. Doubt, that's all. But it won't win. It can't win.

It used to be really different. My bros were the greatest. There was beer and bikes and broads and bros. There was nothing we couldn't handle. Together. I mean, it was more fun that way. Together. People respected us. They better, man. That's how it was. We feared nothing. We took no crap off anyone. Even the broads. There were always more.

So how in hell did this happen? Because I wanted it. There is nothing to do and too much to do at the same time. And there's this little crawling...doubt. The others up here, they must be scared out of their minds, man. They laugh when they come by, but they don't fool me for a minute. I mean, this country is the pits. There is nothing to do but look at the snow and the trees and the ice and cut firewood. The others are crazy. That's it.

Well, I'm not crazy. I can see the country for what it is. The pits. The do-nothing, bored, ever-loving pits, man, and there ain't no other word for it.

You take Sherry. She used to be exciting. Classy little broad, man. Ask the bros. She wasn't no pass-around stuff, either. Married her, too. A good old lady. Went everywhere together. Now look. Wears an apron. Bakes bread, for God's sake! Wants a dog. Next thing you know, she'll want a brat. No way, man.

And she says she *likes* it here. She *likes* it!

It's beautiful, Les. Did you see the sunset, Les? Isn't the snow beautiful, Les? Wouldn't it be fun to have a dog, Les? Can you cut me some more firewood, Les? Don't you think we (we!) could try trapping a bit farther up the creek, Les? The water buckets are getting kinda low, Les. I could use some more stove wood,

Les. Did you see how pretty it is when the snow hangs on the spruce branches, Les? And maybe we could go into the village and have a party, Les?

She'd like that. Go into town, tell everybody she's getting lonely in the woods. They'd laugh. Laugh, man. They think a city man can't whip this country into shape. Hell!

Les, could you maybe split some more of the birch for the cook stove?

It's fine for her to stand over there by the stove and talk. Does she think she's fooling me? Does she think I can't see through her? Just how dumb does she think I am? She thinks I'll get weak, and soft, and want to go back Outside to the bros. She didn't say it, but she thinks it. Oh, she does all right.

"What you thinking, honey?"

"What do *you* care, Sherry?"

"Just wondering, that's all."

"Well, just wonder to yourself. Yes, just wonder to yourself. Now is when you are supposed to tell me the damn woodpile is down again, isn't it, Sherry? Isn't the damn woodpile low again?"

"Well..."

"Well, well? Well, Miss Woodsman, why the hell don't you get your own ass in gear and go out and cut some for a change, huh? All you do is yell at me about it. OK. So you don't yell, but you whimper, yes, whimper like a dumb broad. Oh, that's it, cry. That's the answer, cry. Well, you can just do your crying outside while you cut some of the damned wood around here. You want it warm in here? You want to bake the bread in here? You want to burn up that wood around here? Then go out and cut it yourself for a change."

"Les, I..."

"Oh, let's see, now. It's going to be the tears and the poor me, I'm just a woman, and you're the big strong man, and I can't carry those heavy pieces of wood. Well, lady, you can just get the hell outa here!"

"I didn't mean..."

"Out! Go on, get out there and cut the damned wood. What's wrong with you? Go!"

His coffee cup missed her by inches, and the coffee splattered against the long wall.

• • •

A cold snap affects everyone. By the second week, several notable things had happened in the village.

In the trading post, Minnie Hunter spent more time listening to the radio than talking with the customers. She hung up a sign saying "Absolutely No Credit," which everyone ignored. It would be taken down in the spring, as it was each spring.

John Thompson and Siwash Simmons weren't speaking. They had gotten into an argument at the South Seas one night about which was farther north, Oregon or Mongolia. Neither wanted to look it up, so it was easier not speaking.

Mary Davis cried each morning when Buck flew, her mind filled with plane crashes. In some daydreams she saw the big jet flown by her son slam into a mountain. In others, it was Buck's aircraft that stalled in a steep climb, failed to clear a rocky ridge, or overshot the runway. Her housework suffered. She didn't put on any makeup in the evenings, even though she knew it pleased Buck to see her wearing lipstick.

King Cabin Fever reigned in the community and in the surrounding bush. It would take a warming trend and a snowfall to end the rule, and there was absolutely nothing anyone could do about it. Even the disc jockeys in Anchorage began to complain about the weather from their warm electronic cubicles. The songs on the radio seemed sadder than usual, the front page of the newspaper more depressing.

"Why do you put so much sugar in your coffee?" Mary Davis asked Buck one morning.

"I always put sugar in my coffee," he grumbled.

"But not this much. Isn't my coffee any good?"

"It's a little bitter, that's all."

Mary began to cry and Buck stood and put his arms around her. "Honey, it's this weather, that's all. You make good coffee. You have always made good coffee. It's this damn weather."

Mary nodded on his shoulder, but continued crying.

"It's just this damn weather," he said.

"Cabin fever, huh?"

"Yeah, on everybody."

"You flying today, Buck?"

"Thought about it."

"Do something for me?"

"Sure. What?"

"Check on those kids out at Lynx Lake, OK? I'm worried about that girl."

"That Sherry's OK, Mary. It's her husband that's likely to go bananas."

Mary wiped her eyes and smiled up at her husband.

"That's why I'm worried about the girl."

"I'll stop in this afternoon. First thing. OK?"

"Want more coffee?"

"Sure do."

• • •

Frank Granger stopped by the trading post on his way back from the post office.

"Mornin' Minnie. Cold as hell out there."

"You bet, Frank. Want some coffee?"

"No time. Just need some shaving soap."

Minnie Hunter reached behind her and lifted down a box of old-fashioned shaving soap. Frank was the only person who ever bought it, and she had never questioned why he preferred it to pressurized lather. She simply kept a supply of it for him.

"That be all today, Frank?"

"Yes. No. I'll take a couple of postcards, too."

"Winter or summer?"

"Winter."

"The village or the mountain?"

"Village. Got one with moose on it?"

"Cow and calf or bull?"

Frank thought for a minute.

"Bull, I guess."

"Trying to scare someone off, Frank?"

Frank looked at her and smiled sadly. "Do you know everything in this village, Minnie?"

She laughed. "Not everything, Frank. Call it woman's intuition." Frank looked at the postcards, hesitating for a minute.

"That offer for coffee still good, Minnie?"

"Sure, Frank. Sit down by the stove and I'll get it."

Frank sat by the big Ashley heater and glanced idly through the outdoor magazines on the table. Some were fifteen years old. They were better than the ones today, he thought. Today it was all paid expeditions using campers, international flights and paid guides. These days it was variable scopes, ballistic tables and pounds of energy at the muzzle. And fishing. Fishing had become more of a scientific endeavor than an art. Silent electric motors pushed a $10,000 boat to a spot where the sonar fish finder said the fish were. A thermometer reading of water temperature dictated what type of lure to use, also taking into account the stages of the moon and the time of day.

Hunting and fishing used to be fun.

Minnie Hunter returned with the coffee and sat down by Frank. "Thanks, Minnie. You have any sugar?"

"Two in it already."

"You remembered?"

"Sure. Who else in the village would die from diabetes if he stirred his coffee?"

Frank looked a bit sheepish.

"Well, I do like a bit of sugar."

Minnie sipped her coffee and watched the tall old man sitting in silence.

"Something wrong, Frank? You're not usually this quiet."

"Oh, no, Minnie. Nothing's wrong. I just wanted to ask you why you live here."

"It's my home."

"Well, sure it is. I guess, you know, you have the kids and grandkids and all that. Did you ever wish you lived Outside?"

"Only during a cold snap like this one, or maybe during breakup when the mud gets bad."

"But you don't go."

"No. No, I don't go."

"You can afford it, Minnie."

"Maybe. Never really thought of it much. This is my home. Say, you trying to get rid of me, Frank Granger?"

"Oh no, gosh, Minnie, I never meant…"

Minnie Hunter laughed. "I think I know what you're getting at, Granger. You mean, what's a lady like me doing in a jerkwater village like this. Right?"

"Yeah, sorta. I mean, you do have options. You could do other things."

"This is my home, Frank. I have children and grandchildren here. I was married here. I have a husband buried here. And I have friends here. Friends may be the real reason anyway. I feel needed here. And, I love the country."

"You really love the country? I mean, being a woman and all?"

"You think this country is just for you he-men?"

Frank laughed. "No. It's just that I never thought a woman could really enjoy this bush country."

"It sure isn't boring, is it?"

"Sure isn't, Minnie. I never knew you felt that way about the country."

"You never asked before, Frank."

"I guess maybe I didn't. Hey, thanks for the coffee. Come on over and I'll return the favor, OK?"

"Sure. Stay warm."

Frank smiled. "You do the same, Minnie. You do the same. Say, you need firewood or anything?"

Minnie shook her head. "Thanks, Frank. My grandson takes care of that."

"Oh. Right. Well, thanks again, Minnie. See ya."

Minnie watched him pull into his parka and mittens and leave the store.

"See ya, Frank. See ya," she said, going to check the prices on wool socks. Then she wrote down the price of Frank Granger's items on his ticket and put it back in the drawer.

"He forgot again," she said, then smiled.

• • •

An observant visitor to a cabin can tell many things about the person who lives there. A look at the shelf of few and precious books can be revealing. Other things, too: the size of the woodpile, cleanliness of the stove, neatness of the clothes, power of the radio, what type of art work hangs on the wall; all are clues.

These generally run to form, and are at least consistent with the different types of people. A person who is slothful is generally consistent in his sloth. An industrious person can generally be spotted by his trappings.

A cabin, by its nature, is even more personal than a house. A house is just a house, when it is located in or near a town. Many different types of people may live in the same house at various times, with very few changes appearing in the house.

A cabin, on the other hand, is more like a suit of clothes. By necessity it is small. Small areas are easier to keep warm. Being small, a cabin requires constant care. Everything must have its place. A log cabin must be swept at least once a day, as it collects dust and dirt.

When one cabin is lived in by two very different people, and the confinement during a cold snap becomes acute, the little log structure takes on a dissonance, a clash in personalities. The cabin itself reflects the attitudes of its inhabitants.

The little cabin at Lynx Lake was suffering.

Sherry had been reared to be a neat housekeeper. Les was a slob. No sooner had she picked one thing up than he had thrown something else down. She longed for him to leave the cabin, if only for an hour, so she could clean. But he just sat and gave orders, and he argued with her, and threw things to the floor. Then he yelled at her for keeping a sloppy house.

So, true to the spirit of cabin fever, Sherry began to keep a sloppy house. When she had finally surrendered to the dissonance of this life, she began to hate herself. She felt Les was right about her, and she pitied him and began to hate him, all at the same time. And she especially hated herself. She couldn't understand the personality change in Les since they had moved to the Bush.

And if Les were the kind of man who could sift things and arrange them in their places, if he had been able to stand back and look objectively at the situation, he would have found he didn't think very much of himself, either.

When Sherry asked him to shovel the snow off the roof, there was a good reason for it. But it had been Sherry's idea, and therefore he wouldn't do it. No woman was about to dictate how he lived. And she could continue to bring in the firewood, too. Sherry was not as strong as Les, though, and had to spend more than an hour each day cutting firewood, splitting it and bringing it in. He had certain pangs, way down deep, about seeing her struggling through the cold with armloads of wood, but denied their existence. His response was to complain if dinner was late.

The trap line didn't suffer. By this time, it didn't exist. After the last snowfall, even the marking ribbons on the trees showing where the traps were set had been buried.

There are just two things that can conquer cabin fever in the Alaska woods in winter: laughter and work. The little cabin at Lynx Lake had neither.

This morning the argument had been about the fire, as usual. Sherry wanted dry spruce for kindling. Dry spruce was hard to find, and Les did nothing about getting it. The fire had to be started with green birch, and that takes a long time. The coffee isn't ready until the fire gets hot. Sherry had not yet learned the old trick of placing the next day's kindling in the oven to kiln-dry it for the morning fire. These things take time, experimentation, and exposure to veterans of the forest, and the Douglas family had none of these, either.

Les complained about the fire. Sherry countered by complaining about his unwillingness to cut wood. Les said he needed coffee. Sherry stood there and began to talk in a quiet, controlled voice, but what she said was devastating. She said Les was a sadist, a spineless cripple, a hopeless moron, a lazy slob. She recalled every single opportunity he had to do something around the cabin and hadn't. She remembered every time he had said he was going to run the trap line, and didn't.

Les slapped her.

Then, with her sobbing quietly, Les told her how he could have picked any one of several broads for a wife, but had done her the honor, and what did it get him? A chronic complainer. A nag. A lazy slut of a wife who didn't want to pull her share, who wouldn't know how to take care of a mountain man if she had to.

It was still dark outside the cabin, and the light shone through the window. In the yard, several gray jays picked at the brown snow where the dishwater had been thrown. They picked up their heads when the voices got loud. They listened, even as the sun began its pinkish journey to the south. In full daylight, they flew to the trees when the crashing and thrashing began inside the cabin, the shouts and yells of the male voice punctuated by the sobbing moans of the female voice.

The birds tilted their heads in curiosity when the voices both rose to screams. The birds flew away from the cabin at the sound of the rifle shot.

chapter 18

BUCK ENJOYED the weather from inside the warm 185. The bitter cold also brought with it clear blue skies, uncluttered views of the mountain ranges, and a feeling of well-being.

He fished the harmonica out of his pocket and serenaded the engine as he skimmed high above the frozen lakes and the locked-in forests of the area.

On the ice of Lynx Lake, a splash of red caught his eye, and he swung the big plane down for a closer look. It was a space blanket, red side up for emergency. He circled and saw a parka-clad figure step slowly out of the cabin and stare up at the sky.

He landed quickly and had barely left the plane when Sherry ran up and threw herself into his arms, clinging in a bone-crushing hug and sobbing.

They walked up to the cabin in silence, and she pulled away from him at the door and stood crying while he went in.

Buck looked at the scene as though he were someone else. There was nothing businesslike about him as he looked. Nothing was catalogued; nothing was explained. A man lay dead on the floor.

A woman, girl, really, was crying outside.

Then Buck saw the smashed coffee cups and plates. He saw the chair leg broken off, and the shattered window. He went quickly back outside and took the girl in his arms.

"It's OK, Sherry. It's over."

"I didn't mean it, Buck. I didn't want to…"

"It was an accident, girl, anybody can see that."

"No," she shook her head and drew herself up. "No, it wasn't an accident."

Buck took the girl in his arms again and used her parka ruff to wipe the tears off her face.

"Listen to me, Sherry. It was an accident. It happened. That's all. I know what happened, and you know what happened. In a way, your husband committed suicide."

"But Buck…"

"There is more than one way of committing suicide. Sometimes we can simply start down a road that can lead only to tragedy. That's as much committing suicide as taking an overdose of pills or hanging yourself in the woods."

"I did it, Buck, I had to, but…"

He tilted her chin up until she was staring squarely at his cold eyes.

"You are going to go get in that airplane now and wait for me. Do you understand?"

She nodded weakly.

"Then we are going to fly to town. And when we are in town, the trooper will ask questions. And you are going to say that you were out getting wood when you heard the shot."

"But…"

"You were out getting wood when you heard the shot."

"Buck!"

"You were *out getting wood* when you heard the shot!"

She nodded, too weak to object.

He hugged her closely.

"Sherry, honey, one life is gone. OK? Does it make sense to ruin another one? Now listen. We both know what happened, and we know that it was coming, and that it couldn't be helped. Right?"

She nodded.

"Go get in the plane."

Buck walked into the cabin, pulled the rifle from under the body of Lester Douglas, and checked it. He emptied the magazine and ejected the spent shell from the chamber. He fingered every part of the rifle, took out the bolt and put it in his pocket, and leaned the rifle against the door.

Buck rolled the body over and stood looking at it for a minute. Then he brought in a tarp from the woodpile and rolled Douglas's body into it. With the body over his shoulder and the rifle in his hand, he walked slowly and heavily out to the airplane. Sherry looked up at him with vacant eyes.

"Shouldn't we leave him here until, I mean…"

Buck shoved the body into the cargo cavity behind the seats, followed by the rifle.

"Sherry," he said, "you just remember you were outside getting wood when you heard the shot."

"Yes, Buck."

Trooper Macklin stood staring at the large map on the wall, his eyes zeroing in on Lynx Lake. His hands twitched nervously. Sherry Douglas was crying quietly, with Buck's arm around her.

"Mrs. Douglas," Macklin said, his back still to her, "there will be a statement to sign, and there may be more questions later, but probably not. Thank you for coming in. You can go now."

They rose to leave the office.

"Like a word with you alone, Buck," Macklin said.

"You go wait in the car with Mary," Buck told Sherry, watching her walk out and into the arms of his wife.

When the door shut, Macklin turned around slowly and stared at Buck Davis.

"Just what in the hell do you think you're doing, Davis?"

"What do you mean, Bob?"

"What do I mean? What do I mean?"

Trooper Macklin sat down at his desk and stared straight across it at the innocent face of the bush pilot.

"You sit there, after twenty-some-odd years of experience in handling bush people, including dead bush people, and you get that stupid look on your face, and you have the nerve to ask me what I mean? OK, I'll lay it out for you, Buck."

Macklin held up his fingers as he counted.

"One, messing up the scene of the crime. Two, transporting the body before an investigation was made. Three, handling the firearm in such a way as to eliminate the possibility of checking for fingerprints. I could probably learn enough about this to put you away for giving out legal advice without belonging to the Alaska Bar Association!"

"Aw gee, Bob."

"Aw gee, Bob! How about digging your toe in the sand and hanging your head! Hell, thanks to you, we'll never know exactly what happened out there now. Or, maybe it's just me that'll never know. Is that it, maybe?"

Buck was silent.

"What is it with you, Davis? I mean, do you consider this portion of Alaska your private domain, your kingdom? Don't you realize there are laws we all have to live by? Well, there are, and they were made by smarter men than you and me, and we all damn well have to live by them. I just have this nagging feeling that the boonies here are run by Buck Davis, Dashing Boy Aviator, and the troopers are just supposed to sit here and do paperwork, and escort drunks home from the South Seas Roadhouse. Am I right?"

"Of course not, Bob."

"Well, it seems that way to me, Buck. You know better than to move anything in a case like this. Especially in a case like this. Hell, for all I know, this girl plugged her old man herself. For all I know, the guy had it coming. For all I know, she was outside when she heard the shot, and Douglas was shot by a squirrel who just happened to be in the neighborhood! Am I coming through at all, Buck?"

Buck nodded.

"Well, hell. This death will be listed officially as a self-inflicted accidental gunshot death. It will have to be, that's all. It won't be the first time in this area, and it probably won't be the last. That's all."

"Thanks, Bob."

"Before you go, Buck. This Douglas, was he the guy I heard about with the tied-down gunfighter rig?"

"That's the one."

"All kinds, huh, Buck?"

"All kinds, Bob."

"Look after that girl, will you?"

"Figured on it, Bob."

The trooper turned back to the map and stared at Lynx Lake as he heard the door shut behind Buck.

chapter 19

SHERRY DOUGLAS was taller than Mary Davis, and the kitchen was small, but they seemed to work smoothly together.

Buck scratched his head and smiled over at Sam, who was home again for a few days.

In the time Sherry had stayed with them, she had grown close to both Buck and Mary, and when she returned to the cabin the next day, as she was determined to do, it would be like losing a piece of their own family.

Buck remembered the biting words of Bob Mackin, and he thought again, time after time, about what had happened, and the part he had played in it. Was he right? Did he really have the right to do those things? Aren't there much wiser men than he who are entrusted to solve such problems?

But they weren't there. The men who look at situations and make judgments on people and settle problems don't live where the problems are. They don't know what cold and isolation can do to some people. They read law books by the light of fluorescent tubes set in a composition ceiling. They don't read outdoor catalogs by kerosene lamps. They weren't there. They just weren't there.

The doubts woke him up at night occasionally now. Just the night before, he had wakened from a dead sleep and lain with open eyes staring at the patterns the poles made in the ceiling. It wasn't until long minutes later he heard the quiet sobbing in the living room. It was the loneliest sound Buck Davis had ever heard.

Buck had pulled on his robe and moccasins and walked through the darkened living room into the kitchen. He had heated the coffee, poured two cups, and walked over to the couch.

"I make good coffee," he told the girl.

"I'm sorry I woke you, Buck."

"You didn't. I was having a hard time sleeping anyway."

"Was it because, well, because..."

"No," he said gently but firmly, "no, it wasn't. I don't regret it because it was the right decision to make. You know it and I know it."

Sherry wiped her eyes, sat up, and sipped some of the strong coffee.

"Good coffee, Buck."

"We serve only the best here at the Davis Hilton."

"Buck, do you think things will ever be good, I mean, really good, again?"

He put his hand on the back of her neck and gave a friendly squeeze.

"Honey, I don't know how to answer that. Things change all the time, every day. But I do know that just because bad things happen to us, they don't make us bad, too. They can either weaken us or strengthen us. It's up to us, I guess. But I think it will be fine for you. Give it a little time and see."

Sherry put her coffee down and put her arms around Buck's neck.

"I just keep seeing…"

"Of course you do. We all do when these things happen. And someday you and I will sit down and talk about it. We'll talk about everything that happened, and all the bad things. We'll talk about it all one of these days, but now is the time for forgetting and going on."

He could feel her nod on his shoulder.

Giving her a strong hug, he whispered, "You are welcome to stay here, you know. Mary and I, well, we both.. ."

"I know."

"But you want to go back out?"

"I have to."

"I know. Well now, have all the creepies and ghoulies gone for the night?"

She smiled.

"Buck, you make me feel like a little girl again, safe, like when I had a bad dream and my daddy would come in and hold me."

"Sherry, I think that's the nicest thing anyone's ever said to me."

"Thank you."

"Good night, dear."

Buck put down his coffee cup and returned to Mary's side. The crawly things of conscience had been banished from the little house on the airstrip for another night.

The memories of the dreamlike meeting that night flitted through Buck Davis's mind as he watched the women make dinner, but there was something else going through Sam's mind.

Buck looked at Sam from time to time, but picked up few clues. The story of the shooting had spread through Kahiltna, with rumors of cover-up attached. These things would take time to smooth out into a legend. As far as Buck could see, Sherry had two things going in her favor: people who had met Les Douglas couldn't stand him, and people who knew Sherry loved her. To a man, they wanted to believe it was self-inflicted, an accidental shooting. With time, Buck knew, they all would.

Sam had heard the rumors but did not seem to be bothered. He seemed more fascinated.

"How soon till dinner?" Buck asked.

"Starved as usual?" Mary smiled. 'Well, it'll be sooner than usual, with Sherry's help. Honestly, I don't know what I'm going to do without her around here, Buck."

"Oh, go on," Sherry said. "You're just saying that."

"Young lady," Buck said, "I've never known Mary to let another woman fuss around in her kitchen. I think you can take that as being the truth. Am I right, Sam?"

"Huh?"

"Am I right?"

"Oh, sure, dad. Sure."

Buck looked quizzically at the expression on the young jet pilot's face, and chuckled to himself.

"Let's eat, boys."

"All right!"

Sherry found Sam attractive, with the dignity and foursquare bearing of his father, and the large brown eyes of his gentle mother. When he caught her looking at him, her eyes would go down to her plate and study the rivers and canyons and mountain ranges in her slab of moose roast.

Sam was aware of her gaze, and felt guilty because he, too, had been gazing at her through dinner. It was a quiet meal. Afterward Buck got out a bottle of brandy left by some mountain climbers and added a shot to everyone's coffee.

"Special occasion, honey?"

"Can't toast someone with just coffee, Mary. And I want to toast Sherry. No. I want to toast a friendship just starting between us and Sherry, and not just the ending of a visit."

He looked around the table and saw his family nod in agreement and the guest of honor blush.

"This girl blushes worse'n any I've seen," Buck laughed. "Well, honey, here's to you and your cabin on Lynx Lake. May you get tired of it soon, so you'll come back and visit us before we realize you're gone."

"Thank you, thank you very much. I…"

"Buck, you old rascal, you made the girl cry!"

"Now, Mary, I didn't mean…"

Sherry began to chuckle, even through the tears, and saw Sam join in. Soon all four were laughing.

"Now you see," Buck said, turning to Sam. "You see for yourself the wonders of being a bush pilot. Why, in the course of an ordinary day, I get to make pretty girls cry. Right at my own table. How about it, jet jockey? Is your style of flying that much fun?"

"You might have a point, there, dad," Sam conceded, "but I still don't have to change my own spark plugs."

"Maybe not, but at 30,000 feet you can't enjoy watching the country slip by beneath your wings."

"Very true, very true. But I eat regularly and I can fly that plane in a whiteout."

"Well, I can fly a plane in a whiteout, too!"

"Yes, you can, dad. I'll admit that, but I can land mine, too."

Buck laughed and Sherry chuckled, and only Mary showed little signs of hurt and fear around her eyes as she smiled.

Sam was quiet for a minute.

"Dad, maybe I've been stubborn about bush flying."

"You think maybe, huh?"

"Well, maybe I have. Now I was thinking maybe, I mean, since I'm home for a few days and all, and I mean, I know you always need help, well, I thought maybe I'd fly for you tomorrow. If that'd be all right."

"Hmmmm." Buck rubbed his chin and tugged on his ear. "I have to take Sherry to Lynx Lake in the 185, and then fly some stuff out to Otter Creek in the Cub. Which run were you thinking of making?"

"Well," Sam looked embarrassed, "I'm more used to flying the 185."

Buck looked at Sherry.

"Any objections to being flown in tomorrow by a wild jet pilot who thinks anything less than two miles is a short airstrip?"

Sherry smiled. "That's OK with me."

"OK, then. But I warn you, Sam, you might like my kind of flying."

"I'll try to keep an open mind."

• • •

Pulling on his robe, Sam walked quietly out to the kitchen in the darkness. The rays from the yard light across the street fell softly on the sleeping figure of Sherry Douglas on the couch. He looked at her slender, gentle fingers emerging from the sleeves of her long johns and marveled at the beauty of a sleeping woman.

As quietly as possible, Sam heated the coffee. He was startled a moment later.

"Enough there for two cups?"

"Oh, morning, Sherry."

"Morning, Sam."

"Didn't mean to wake you. I like to get up about this time of day."

"So do I. Well, maybe not always get up, but wake up, anyway."

"It's so quiet."

"Yes."

Sam brought the coffee over and sat in the overstuffed chair next to her.

"It's not really time to get up yet. It won't be light for hours."

"I don't mind. Sometimes in the early morning like this, it's nice to just lie awake and think. I've done it ever since I was a little girl."

"What did you think about back then?"

She laughed. "I used to lie there listening to the city noises and pretend I was out here in the Bush. Each horn honk was the scream of a bald eagle, and I pretended the truck motors were bears growling. Pretty silly, I guess."

"Not silly at all," Sam said, sipping his coffee. "You wanted to come up here that long ago?"

"I can't remember when I didn't. Sometimes I'd dream that Uncle Pete had sent for me, and I just had to come up and cook for him. When I was older, I taught myself to cook on wood fires, so I'd know, you know, when I came up. And now, here I am. But somehow it's not the way I thought it would be."

"Well," Sam said brightly, "so what do you think of now in the early morning hours?"

"Peace, I guess. I think of living quietly and just working and watching trees, and not having any problems that can't be solved over a cup of coffee like this."

"I'll get us another cup."

Mary Davis poked her head out of the bedroom, took one quick look, and pulled it back in. Buck woke up when she climbed into bed and snuggled up to him.

"What's up?"

Mary smiled sleepily and kissed his forehead.

"Early morning coffee, honey. Go back to sleep."

chapter 20

IT TAKES TIME to get an outfit together. Meals must be planned weeks in advance. Groceries must be bought in bulk amounts. A shopper must never forget the psychological things, either; paperback books, crossword puzzles, candy, a cake mix, letter-writing paper, and perhaps even a diary.

It took Sherry several hours of travel between the grocery store and the trading post to put together her outfit. The chores were complicated by her having to refuse many cups of coffee with the residents of Kahiltna. It would be safe to say the old-timers of the village had decided to adopt Sherry Douglas.

John Thompson carried a spare Woods Four-Star sleeping bag over to where Sam was gassing up the 185.

"In case she gets caught out on the trap line," he said, and walked away.

Harry Pete, Frank Granger and Siwash Simmons all contributed traps. Siwash added a bottle of homemade mink scent, warning her to open it only out of doors or irreparable harm would come to the air inside her cabin.

In the trading post, when Sherry wasn't watching, Minnie Hunter stuffed three new pairs of wool socks down into the bottom of the box.

The final offering didn't arrive until just before takeoff. Sam was loading the pile of supplies into the 185 when Buck walked up behind the aircraft. At a signal from Buck, Siwash attracted Sherry's attention and turned her away from the plane as he explained the finer points of beaver trapping.

Buck whispered to Sam and handed him a lumpy pillowcase. Sam grinned and set it gently into the rear of the plane.

After kisses and tears with Mary and hugs from Buck, Sherry finally strapped herself into the plane. Sam kicked the engine over, and they thundered down the airstrip and flew north toward Lynx Lake.

As they flew, movement below them caught Sherry's eye, and she grabbed Sam's elbow and pointed.

"Moose!"

He nodded.

Over the noise of the engine, Sherry leaned close and said, "It's too bad you're not a real bush pilot."

"What do you mean?" he asked indignantly.

She laughed. "You don't have a harmonica!"

Sam landed skillfully on the lake.

Sherry stood outside the plane looking at the cabin while Sam unloaded the gear.

"Sam, would you mind walking up to the cabin with me?"

"You don't even have to ask."

"Thanks."

The last item unloaded was the pillowcase Buck had given Sam just before takeoff.

"I think you'd better check this out, Sherry. A little present from Buck."

When the pillowcase was opened, a little husky pup peeked out.

"Oh!...Oh!"

Sherry laughed and hugged the little pup until the tears came, then she put him down and he bounced up to her and chewed at the laces on her mukluks.

"I love him. Isn't he beautiful?"

"Mighty handsome pup, that one."

They walked up the rise to the cabin, followed by the pup, and Sam opened the cabin door and walked in. He stuck his head out.

"No bears. Come on in."

Sherry walked in. The cabin was spotless. Even the broken windowpane had been replaced.

"How?"

"Buck and Siwash came up for a picnic the other day."

Sherry's hands shook as she stood looking down at the floor. "How about building a fire and fixing us some coffee?"

"Sure. Oh, I'm sorry, Sam. Of course."

Sam looked around at the cabin and felt a burning grudge against a man he had never met and who was dead. For the next few hours he cut and split wood, shoveled snow off the roof, and repaired the broken hinges on the front door. He split nearly half a cord of stovewood, putting all of his hostilities into each swing of the splitting maul.

"You're not leaving me much to do when you're gone."

Sam stopped splitting wood and grinned.

"I imagine you'll find plenty to do."

"Well, anyway, it's time for dinner. Hope you like moose steak. Siwash gave it to me."

"I probably shouldn't stay."

"Please."

He nodded and went in.

"I guess since I hauled the stuff out here, it's only right that I eat some of it."

"Absolutely. And you can run the puppy out of that cupboard over there by your foot, too."

"He needs a name."

"Any suggestions?"

"I'll think on it and let you know."

Sherry smiled and served the dinner.

As they finished dinner, the puppy nested on a sack next to the stove, and Sam was trying to think of what to say.

"Sherry."

"Yes, Sam?"

"Well, you know, this is quite a job out here."

She smiled teasingly, "For a woman, you mean?"

"Now, that's not what I meant, it's just…"

"I'll be all right, Sam."

Sam looked at her for a long moment, then stood and paced across the tiny cabin.

"OK. What's the best way to trap marten?"

Sherry smiled, then answered without hesitation.

"Use No. 2s in a straight line up a hillside from the bottom to the top. They travel across the hills rather than down the ridges, and they're bound to come across one. Use a piece of ptarmigan for bait, and check the traps often."

"How will you know when you've taken enough beaver out of an area?"

"The rule of thumb is always to leave three beaver to each lodge. That way, I'll never run out of them. I've also decided to skip every other beaver pond for insurance. I'll rig drown sets on them just below ice level."

"Can you shoot?"

"I can hit that tomato can two out of three times at a hundred yards with iron sights."

"Sherry, you're quite a lady. You know that?"

Sherry blushed and poured more coffee. Sam looked up at the sky through the window.

"The light's going."

"Will you be coming by here anytime this winter?"

Sam looked at her shyly. "I thought maybe I'd stop by and do a little ice fishing from time to time."

"You do that."

Sam shrugged into his parka, picked up the pup and hugged it, then stood awkwardly by the door.

"Sherry, I just wanted to say…"

She smiled and held out her hand. He took it and they looked at each other.

"I've heard the ice fishing is good in this lake, Sam."

"That's what I heard, too."

"Thanks for the ride."

"Thanks for the meal."

She stood shivering in the open doorway, watching as he started the plane and flew back toward the village. Then she picked up the puppy in her arms and closed the door on the twilight of her first night alone in the bush.

chapter 21

THE AIRSTRIP was on the left side of the road Siwash Simmons drove, so it was just easier to drive down the left side to get there. Saved gas and tires.

The only oncoming traffic was Minnie Hunter in her new four-wheel drive pickup, and she waved and drove down the wrong side of the road herself, to avoid a misunderstanding.

Buck was gassing up the plane at the pumps across from the South Seas when Simmons drove up in Buck's car with his supplies.

"I hope you didn't drive all the way over here on that side of the road."

"Oh no. Just since the curve. Seemed easier."

Buck shook his head and grinned as Siwash unloaded his supplies into a pile beside the plane. But unloading supplies can be tiring work, and Siwash found it necessary to medicate himself slightly between each of the heavier loads. He was surprised at how many of them were heavy.

It was during one of these breaks that the old trapper noticed a number of people heading for the South Seas Roadhouse as though drawn by a magnet. The number of Kahiltna residents that could be counted on to partake of a morning hour was well-known by him, and this group far exceeded the normal amount.

"What's going on in there, Buck?"

"Beats me."

"Haven't seen that many people in the South Seas since Frank imported that belly dancer from Anchorage."

Spotting John Thompson heading for the bar, Simmons inquired about this midmorning phenomenon. Thompson whispered something.

Siwash's eyes widened, "Strawberries?"

"Yep."

"Hemingway?"

"Yep."

"Real strawberries?"

"Fresh."

Siwash dropped a gunnysack and walked over with Thompson to the roadhouse. The crowd had gathered around the horseshoe-shaped bar and stood staring as Hemingway Jones sprinkled sugar on a salad bowl full of fresh strawberries.

"By golly," Siwash whispered, "you're right."

"Tiny but luscious pearls of the southland," Hemingway said loudly, "deliciously scented by Nature. Drenched in the waftings of the subtropics..."

"Hey, Hemingway," Siwash said, "are those real strawberries?"

"Ah, indeed they are, Mr. Simmons, sir. Freshly picked and air freighted directly to this poor mortal by friends in California of such inestimable esteem that..."

Siwash looked around the room at the drooling people.

"Well, aren't you going to share them?"

"Share them? My dear friend, some things are meant to be shared one way, some another. Of course I mean to share these gems of the warmer climes. Each bite I take, I promise to explain, in detail, the wonderful succulence of these strawberries. You will taste them with me, in spirit."

"Why, you selfish goat!"

Laughter followed Siwash back into the street and across the way to the airstrip. Buck was finishing the loading.

Siwash stood looking back at the South Seas with longing, then looked at Buck. His mouth began to twitch, and any one of Simmons' oldest friends would take cover at that much warning.

"Buck, I got an idear." He whispered to Buck, which brought a sly smile to the bush pilot's face.

"I'll be ready, Siwash."

Simmons walked back over to the South Seas and saw a lineup of youngsters peering in through the windows, standing in knee-deep snow.

Calling one over, he whispered to the kid, who nodded. Then Siwash took a dollar bill and stuffed it into the kid's pocket. The kid shook hands solemnly with Siwash and then walked quietly around behind the South Seas.

"I'm glad you're all here," Hemingway said, as Siwash slipped back into the roadhouse. "I'm glad you're here to witness this, the first bite of strawberries. Strawberries, firm and plump and ruby red from the far southland. True harbingers of spring they are, jetted here at great expense and bother by two of the dearest friends this man has ever known."

Siwash elbowed his way up front for a closer view of the strawberry bowl.

"Yes, friends," Hemingway continued, "even as I take this bite, I do it for all of us, knowing as I do so, I taste this for us all. I enjoy the aroma for us all. I savor the syrupy..."

"Help! Help! Oh, help, he's got me! Come quick! Oh help!"

The screams from behind the roadhouse sent twenty men, Hemingway Jones included, out the back door to rescue the youngster in distress.

Only Siwash Simmons used the front door. Very quickly. With the strawberries.

Hemingway took one glance at the boy, and screamed his woes as terrible thoughts came to his mind. He dashed back to the strawberries only to find them gone, and raced out the front door after the fleeing trapper.

Siwash Simmons would never make anyone's track team, especially in parka and mukluks, but he had too much of a lead to be caught short of the airplane.

Buck had the plane facing down the runway, engine revving loudly, when he spied the broken-field running of the potbellied old-timer coming up behind.

Hemingway was closing on the trapper when he reached the plane, shouting curses at him every step. Simmons found running to be painless when in possession of such a treasure, and his adrenaline took him onto the moving ski of the aircraft in record time. He passed the bowl of strawberries in to Buck, then scrambled into the aircraft and closed the door behind him before the plane left the ground.

Left in a hurricane of propwash-driven snow, Hemingway Jones was seen to jump and yell and say improper things at the departing airplane.

Buck turned the plane around and headed back over the airstrip in a bush pilot's strafing run, and Hemingway looked up to see one of his beloved strawberries disappear into a grinning beard as it swept past.

The plane disappeared over a ridge out of town with a happy wagging of wings, and the laughing crowd dispersed.

Siwash was laughing, too.

"You shoulda heard the speech that selfish booger was giving the crowd. Oh, you'd have laughed, all right."

Buck grinned. "Siwash, give me one of those big ones down by the bottom."

"Now Buck, these leetle biddy ones are more tasty."

"You wanta get out and walk?"

"One great big one coming up!"

The level of strawberries in the bowl diminished with each air mile covered during the flight. Finally there was only a residue of sugar at the bottom.

"Buck, my friend, life ain't nothing but a great big bowl of strawberries."

"You are so-o-o right!"

And the laughter soon gave way to a harmonica rendition of "Jinny Git Around."

chapter 22

THE COMB was a killer. The wind began early in the afternoon, and no pitons could give the trio of climbers any semblance of security.

As usual, Cruchot led. As usual, it was Morris, the businessman, who indicated they should make camp soon. Hunter tried to keep peace between the two, and find something worthwhile each day they spent on the mountain. It wasn't always easy.

For three days they had had to make a hammock camp on the vertical face of the Comb. Pitons would be driven into crevices in the rock face, and hammocks slung between them. The packs, for the most part, swung from a free rope far below. They were hauled up hand over hand only as the need demanded.

Cruchot was angry. There were still two hours of daylight left when Morris motioned he wanted to make camp. Two hours. Morris had spotted a tiny flaw in the Comb, a tiny pocket filled with ice that was nearly level and nestled between two knife ridges of rock. The pocket was just over five feet wide and nearly ten feet deep. In another hour, Morris would be up to the pocket. In it, he saw the opportunity to sleep in a tent for the night, out of the wind.

When climbing the massif, adventurers learn that comfort is a relative matter. If a man has been standing in bright desert sun for hours, the relative shade of a straw hat seems like an oasis. Similarly, a mountain climber who has spent three nights swaying in the wind while suspended in a hammock some 4,000 feet above a frozen rock pile finds a near-level patch of ice tucked in a cliff to be a secure fortress against the elements.

Cruchot was first to reach the lip curling over into the niche. He set about securing the ropes going down to Hunter and Morris. Then he hauled up the packs slowly, hand over hand, and had the single three-man tent pitched by the time the other two arrived.

Morris was pulled the last few feet by Hunter, and fell onto a bare patch of ice above the tent. He was breathing very hard, but smiling.

Cruchot looked at Hunter. "You cook tonight."

"Sure thing."

Morris caught his breath and looked around at the tiny niche they occupied.

"Beautiful. Just beautiful. Look at this, gentlemen. A night out of the wind. We should have brought a deck of cards along to celebrate our security."

Hunter grinned and began pulling things out of the packs. Cruchot, the stubble on his face coated with frost, rubbed his face clean with climbing mittens and stared at Morris.

"Well, fat man, I hope you are happy. We are at a little more than 17,000 feet, with 3,000 more to go, and we're short of food. I hope the view is pleasant for you, sir. It may be as high on this mountain as we'll get."

"Well, what's wrong with that?" replied Morris. "You said yourself we didn't have enough food to make the summit, right? OK, let's take our time, and enjoy the climb we've made."

Cruchot didn't answer, but disappeared inside the tent with his sleeping bag, followed by the others.

The puffing stove warmed the tent, and the men were able to get by with only the silk inner gloves that evening. From their sleeping bags, they wrote in their journals. Cruchot finished first, stepped outside the tent for the necessaries, and hurried back inside.

"Bad night on the Comb," he said.

"Wind?"

"Yes."

"How about tomorrow?" Hunter asked.

"Up to Morris."

"Up to me? How do you figure that?"

"Number one, you are the slowest member of this climbing team, if you can call it that. Therefore, we must all go as slowly as you do. Number two, you eat more than Hunter and I combined, which means our groceries are nearly gone."

Cruchot looked over at the astonished Morris.

"Number three, I do not, my friend, think that you can climb mountains. Or that you want to climb mountains. It is all a how-you-say, picnic. Am I correct?"

"You got me wrong, Andre," Morris said, "No, no, sir, you have it all wrong. I like to climb. What did we just climb, anyway, some playground equipment?"

"He's right," Hunter agreed. "We just climbed a 4,000-foot rock wall in winter, Cruchot. Not shabby."

"Not shabby!" If Cruchot could have stood, he would have paced. "OK, we climbed a difficult wall. That's OK as far as that goes, but we're still nearly a mile below the summit. Straight below the summit. And it might as well be ten miles, the way things are now."

"It's not that bad, Cruchot."

"Worse, maybe, Hunter. Consider this for a minute. If the weather was good, if our friend Morris here was a climber and didn't have twenty extra pounds of fat, if we had enough food to last us, then we could reach the summit in another three days. If we took the easy way down the West Buttress to get off, that's still another five days, minimum. But we don't have those conditions. I'm trying to be reasonable about this, Hunter, but this fellow is getting to bother me, and I don't care if he does have all the money."

"Is that why you wanted me along?"

Hunter punched Morris playfully on the shoulder. "Of course not, Big Mo. Cruchot is just upset right now, that's all."

Cruchot looked coldly at Morris. "Morris, you were invited along because an expedition like this costs money. Hunter didn't have the money. I didn't have the money. You have the money. Simple."

Hunter looked shocked. "Andre…"

"It's OK, kid," Morris said with a weak smile. "So you invited me along for the money. That's fine with me. So the big question is, what do we do now?"

Hunter and Morris looked at the veteran climber.

"Well, hell, I don't know. Dammit! I wanted to make that summit!"

Hunter pulled out a favorite bulldog pipe, filled it with Sir Walter Raleigh, and lit his evening pipe.

"Getting mad isn't going to help."

"Do you have to smoke that damn thing every night?"

"Yes, Cruchot," Hunter said coolly, "I do."

Morris just smiled.

"OK," Hunter continued, "let's take a close look at our options at this point. We're not in the very choicest of circumstances at the moment. We cannot continue up the Comb, and we can't go back down the face, as that would take too long. Am I right so far?"

Cruchot nodded.

"OK. Can we traverse to the left and get on the West Buttress, then reach the summit from there?"

Cruchot brightened. "I never thought of that."

"But it's possible?"

"Possible? Yes."

"I suppose it depends on the food supply?"

"And the weather."

"The weather. Right. But anyway, if we traverse over to the West Buttress, we can decide then whether to try for the summit. And if we don't go for the top, at least we'll be in a better position to descend, right?"

"That's true." Cruchot brightened a little and fired up the stove for tea. "The only thing is, we have climbed more than halfway up the Comb. If we traverse over to the buttress, we will have climbed this far for nothing."

Morris looked aghast. "For nothing?"

"For absolutely nothing. The Comb has been climbed before in summer. French party years ago. The mountain was climbed before in winter by Genet, Johnston and Davidson, using the West Buttress. We would have to climb to the summit on the Comb to make this climb an official seasonal first."

...

Morris collapsed shortly before noon the following day.

The difficult traverse across the face had been made in less than three hours, and the trio of climbers had faced a steep but not vertical ascent.

Above was the peak, its rounded mound of snow shining brightly in the winter sun. The day was perfect; cold, but without the heavy winds of the day before.

Morris had just suddenly sat down along the knife edge, and wouldn't move. Hunter and Cruchot had hurried to him, but were unable to get an answer from him. The older man sat with his head between his knees, gasping for breath.

Hunter shook Morris by the shoulder.

"What's the matter, Big Mo, you in pain?"

Morris shook his head, but could not speak.

Cruchot knelt by Morris.

"Lift your head a minute, Morris. Not good. Not good at all." Cruchot turned to speak to Hunter. "See how his lips are starting to turn blue? He's starting to sweat, too."

Hunter looked carefully at the stricken man.

"What's the matter with him, Andre?"

"Altitude sickness, pulmonary edema. What happens is the heart overworks trying to get enough oxygen to the blood."

"How bad is it?"

"We have to get him down," said Cruchot, "that's how bad it is. We have to get him to a lower elevation, fast."

"Serious?"

"He could die if we don't. I've seen it happen."

Hunter spoke softly to Morris.

"Can you walk at all, Big Mo?"

"I don't think so."

Cruchot looked down the mountain. Below them was a steep drop of nearly 2,000 feet to the head of a glacier.

"Can we get down there quickly, Andre?"

"We have to, my friend, we have to."

With the tent pulled from the haul bag, they jury-rigged a toboggan of sorts for Morris. First they tried laying him flat on it, but Morris began to choke for air, and violently pulled himself back up into a sitting position.

"If we wrap that nylon tent around him, I think he'll slide," Hunter said.

"He has to," agreed Cruchot.

Hunter looked down the mountain at the head of the glacier. "How far down do we have to take him?"

"Maybe 4,000 feet. I don't really know what those airplanes can do. We'll get him down there and then call."

Rigging ropes with nonslip knots around Morris, the unlikely trio began the steep descent to the glacier. Hunter went first, feeling ahead with a ski pole for hidden hazards in the loose snow. The panting, crouching Morris, sliding along on the nylon tent, took the middle position. The stronger Cruchot anchored the trio's descent from behind, strong legs digging deep with each step. It was aching work, frantic work, dangerous work, but it took them slowly down the shoulder of the mountain.

chapter 23

WHEN THE COFFEE was done, Mary poured some for herself and Sam. Her son walked to the window and contemplated the sky.

"Good day for flying, honey?"

Sam grinned. "Just looking, Mom. I guess dad made it through the pass OK this morning, but from the looks of those clouds, he won't be back until tomorrow."

"It must be nice not to have to worry about the weather in your work, Sam."

"Oh, we still have to worry about the weather, but not as much, I'll admit. I don't care how many times I've done it, and done it safely, too, Mom. I don't like flying when I can't see."

"You'll be going back soon, I guess."

"Not for a few days yet."

"I've seen you pacing around the past few days, Sam. You must be anxious to get back."

Sam sipped his coffee and stared seriously at his mother. He thought a minute before answering.

"I'm not sure anymore, Mom. The other day, I could see some of the reasons dad flies out here. It has its good points, I guess. When I was flying out to Lynx Lake the other day, I began to get the feel of it. It's kind of like the difference between driving a Greyhound bus and riding a bicycle. A pilot feels a little closer to his craft out here, I guess. And you know, when I was flying, I was thinking about how many moose were in this little valley, or along that creek. I even thought I recognized some marten tracks along Pirate Creek."

Mary smiled. "Do you know what a bush pilot is, really? He's nothing but an old mother hen with an airplane. Look at that map on the wall. See those pins? Each one is a person or a family, friends of your father. Each one is almost totally dependent on Buck to supply the mail and groceries and gas and dog food. Buck keeps a book that's always left here, telling when one of those people plans to come in, or when they may need groceries. It tells which one has a doctor's appointment, or when the baby is due. It has the latest update on the condition of the airstrip at that particular cabin. When someone is due to run short of groceries, and your father is weathered in for several days, he can't sleep. I've seen it time and again. As far as Buck is concerned, those are his people out there. That's what being a bush pilot is all about."

"But why does he leave the book here, Mom? I'd think he'd take it along in the plane with him."

Mary smiled sadly.

"He wants it here in case something should happen to the plane. He'd want me to give it to someone who could keep an eye on his people."

"I think I'll go for a walk."

Blowing steam from beneath his parka hood, Sam smiled and nodded to the neighbors. He seemed to view the village as a three-dimensional photograph, the colors in a friendly blending. He saw the youngest Hunter boy driving a raggy mutt hooked to an American Flyer sled going down to the post office. He noticed the crooked stovepipe on Mike Delaney's cabin. It had been crooked since the earthquake, and Mike had never seemed to get around to fixing it. The neighbors waved and smiled. Frank Granger was coming back from the post office with several letters and a big smile.

It is a good village, Sam thought. It's old and creaky and half unpainted; it's a blend of gold-rush honky-tonk and stucco, dog team and television. It's a good village, and it's home.

• • •

Frank Granger wanted to prolong the pleasure of the letter as much as possible, so he first poured a cup of coffee, adding an extra half-teaspoonful of sugar, then cleared the old newspaper from his favorite table, and grinned widely as he put on his reading glasses and opened the letter with the familiar Minnesota postmark.

"Frank got another one," Harry Pete said, winking to Hemingway. "He'll be in a good mood the rest of the day. Now's the time to hit him up for a raise."

"How about it?" Hemingway laughed. "I could use a bit more money, Frank."

But their teasing stopped when they looked closer at Frank Granger. The color had drained from his face, his mouth hung slack, and he was shaking his head slowly from side to side.

"No," he whispered. "Oh no. Oh, no."

"Frank, are you all right?" Harry asked.

"No, I don't believe it. No. She can't."

Hemingway came around the bar and walked to the table.

"Bad news?"

"Oh no, no, she can't, not now."

"This from that special lady, Frank?"
He nodded absently.
"Found somebody else?"
"No," he mumbled, stunned. "Worse. Much worse."
Hemingway and Harry looked at each other.
"My God, Harry," Hemingway whispered, "I think maybe she died."
"No, boys, not that."
Frank looked up at them with a terrified look on his face.
"She's coming here!"
"Hot damn!" Harry said. "We get to meet her."
'What's so bad about her coming here, Frank?" asked Hemingway. "I thought you liked her."
"I do, boys. I like her very much. Very much. It's hard to explain, but I really wish she wouldn't come. Things would change. It's hard to explain."
"Afraid she'll find out the South Seas isn't exactly the Waldorf?"
"No. I sent her a picture. She knows about the place."
"I know," said Harry. "She thinks you look like Clark Gable."
"Who's Clark Gable?" asked Hemingway. Harry and Frank just looked at him.
"She knows what I look like, too," said Frank.
"Well, look Frank," Harry said. "If you really don't want her to come, why don't you just write and tell her? If she's as nice a lady as you think, she'll respect your wishes."
"You boys don't understand," Frank said, standing uncertainly and folding the letter carefully into the envelope. "You see, she's coming here tomorrow."
"Tomorrow? Here? Oh, hot damn!"
"Harry, this really isn't funny!"
"How's she getting here?"
"She says she'll be here on tomorrow's train, and asked if I would meet her at the train station."
"Train station?" Harry and Hemingway were laughing again. "Now, Frank, don't you think you could make it all the way across the square to our train station tomorrow?"
Kahiltna's train station consisted of a wooden platform for stacking luggage.
"Blue coat," Frank mumbled, heading for the stairs.
"What's that, Frank?"
He looked back at them from a terror-stricken face. "She says she'll be wearing a blue coat."
Frank left the room and climbed the stairs slowly.

Harry Pete grinned and poured another coffee. "Hot damn!" Hemingway said, "Who's Clark Gable?"

• • •

"Davis Air Service, Davis Air Service, this is Cruchot."

"Davis Air Service. Go ahead, Andre."

"Roger. We've got a sick man here, and need a plane out as soon as possible."

"Roger. You have a sick man. What is your location, Cruchot?"

"We're right below the head of the Kahiltna Glacier. Elevation about 14,000 feet."

"Roger. Fourteen thousand on Kahiltna. Have you tested the glacier for crevasses?"

"Roger. Negative on crevasses. We've marked out a strip about 900 feet. Good straight-in approach. When can Buck get in here?"

"Cruchot, what is your weather?"

"Clear and cold here. Almost no wind. Little down-glacier breeze from time to time. Some clouds forming down the canyon."

"Roger on that, Cruchot. Can see the clouds from here. How is your sick man?"

"He's better now. Altitude sickness. But he needs a ride down as soon as possible."

"Roger. Understand. Pack the airstrip well with snowshoes, and put an orange marker at the down-canyon end. Do you copy?"

"Roger. Pack with snowshoes and put a marker at the lower end. We'll start now."

"Andre, I'll see what I can do at this end. Call me back in fifteen minutes. Do you copy?"

"Roger. Will call back in fifteen. Cruchot clear."

"Hang in there. Davis clear."

• • •

Hunter finished tamping the lower end of the glacier landing strip and paused for breath. Down the twisting canyon below, the glacier wound and scoured before widening into a dirty frozen river of crevasses. At this elevation on the mountain, there was only one place a plane could land, and this was it. Above was vertical rock, below were canyons, but here the very start of the more than twenty miles of glacier lay gently sloped in a cul-de-sac of canyon walls. The twin tracks of snowshoes rode up the slope to the orange tent where Morris lay.

Hunter walked back up the length of the airstrip, packing the snow even more on his way. Cruchot sat on a rock ledge above the tent, searching down the canyon with the binoculars.

Hunter checked Morris, who smiled, then climbed up next to Cruchot. "Called them back yet?"

Cruchot nodded. "They're sending a plane right away. It looks like those clouds are closing in down there pretty fast. She said we'll have to load right up and go."

Hunter leaned back against the rock. "Any sign of the plane yet?"

"Not yet. It'll be you and Morris going out. I'll stay here until tomorrow."

"Why?"

"Plane can only get off with two of us, she said. I'll stay here and spend a little time by myself." Cruchot smiled at Hunter. "It won't be so bad for me, you know. I'm not such bad company. I can tell myself some stories."

"Sorry the climb turned out this way, Cruchot."

"Well, so am I. But it was a good scramble up that wall."

Hunter smiled through his cracked and frostbitten face.

"You know, I believe you have the makings of a real human being."

Due to the twisting of the canyon, the men heard the plane a long time before they saw it. When it came, it came in fast, swinging around the bend in the canyon wall, jerking down the flaps and heading for the blaze-orange marker. On this airstrip, there would be no second chance. The plane had to land straight in on the first run, as there wasn't enough room between the canyon walls to turn around.

The plane approached the uphill landing "hot," with an upsurge of power at the last second. The skis touched the snow, and the pilot cut the power and slid to a stop next to the tent. With a roar and blowing snow, the plane spun around facing the downhill-sloping airstrip.

Hunter and Cruchot were at the plane and opening the door before it had stopped its turn.

It was a very nervous Sam Davis who smiled at them, the muscles in his face taut against the skin.

"I'm not going to shut it off. We don't have that much time. Get that sick man in here, and I can take one of you along. Then let's get the hell out of here. The clouds are closing us in."

Morris was helped into the back seat, and Hunter sat up front next to Sam.

Sam reached across Hunter for the door and looked at Andre. "Buck will be in for you tomorrow if the weather is clear. Be ready to go. And stay right here, OK?"

Cruchot nodded in the roar of the propwash.

"OK," Sam yelled. "Now go to the back and hold onto the tailskid while I gun 'er. When you see your partner wave, let 'er go!"

The door was shut and latched, and Cruchot crouched in the frozen propwash of the plane as the engine picked up its roar. Andre found himself sliding, despite his best efforts, and then he saw the wave of the hand and let go.

The big Cessna 185 shot forward, the tail rising immediately. Sam stared ahead and gave it full power. Hunter sat terrified in the passenger seat as he saw the orange marker race up to the hurtling aircraft.

At the end of the airstrip, Sam Davis jerked up on the flap handle, lifting the plane off the snow and sending it flying down the glacier, scant feet off the rough ice. As the plane picked up speed and began to fly, Sam banked it to the right down the canyon. He breathed easier when he saw the glacier dropping farther and farther beneath the skis under them.

Sam took several deep breaths and smiled at Hunter.

"You guys packed a good runway there."

"Little short, wasn't it?"

Sam laughed. "Only on one end, man. Only on one end."

"That was a beautiful takeoff."

"Davis Air Service is always available for beautiful takeoffs, my friend. By the way, I'm Sam Davis. Buck's son."

Hunter introduced himself and shook hands.

"I've been telling Big Mo back here that he'll be OK as soon as we get him lower down," Hunter said, "which goes to show that some people will do anything to keep from walking down a mountain."

Sam looked carefully and long down the canyon at the swirling cloudbanks. "Don't relax just yet, fellas. We still have a few problems to solve."

chapter 24

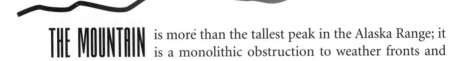

THE MOUNTAIN is more than the tallest peak in the Alaska Range; it is a monolithic obstruction to weather fronts and airplanes.

It is not uncommon for the mountain to play host to two or three cloud layers at once, so from the edge of the village of Kahiltna, looking at the peak, it would appear to have Saturn-like concentric rings climbing its slopes. To the unpracticed observer, it would seem a simple process to fly in the clear air between these layers, land, then fly back out again to clear air. But experienced pilots know these cloud layers for what they really are: temporary.

Within minutes, banks of clouds miles apart can dissipate and vanish, leaving sparkling sky in their places. They also have been known to thicken and come together until there is but one giant cloud, with a mountain in the center. Occasionally these cloud banks can extend, seemingly parallel, then suddenly close together at a distant point. In mountain country, these become the most feared of all cloud formations, referred to by pilots with macabre humor as "cumulogranite" clouds. Many an aircraft has flown into these clouds, never to emerge on the other side.

These images, along with a multitude of weather and flying information, were crowding Sam Davis' thoughts as he flew farther and farther down the Kahiltna Glacier toward the clouds. In the tiny confines of the Cessna, he felt naked. Here he was, in little more than a broad wing with a gasoline engine in front, and almost no instrumentation to steer by. True, the plane had a magnetic compass and an artificial horizon, but little else.

How simple it would be in the jet. Sam knew just what he'd do then. He'd advance the thrust, tilt the nose up and simply climb up to the parts of the sky that hold no mountains, fly on a radio heading to the nearest two-mile runway, and follow the ILS beacon down to the waiting pavement.

Sam checked the fuel gauges with anxiety. There was enough fuel to reach the Kahiltna strip, he knew. He had made certain of that before leaving the village. He had also known that he would never be able to get the airplane to lift off the snow at 14,000 feet with full tanks, so had taken barely enough gas to make the flight, and little more.

The breeze blowing down the mountain met at the base with onshore winds coming from distant Cook Inlet, and the clouds were boiling up the canyons, whipped and opaque like mashed potatoes, up and up, high and higher in front of the tiny plane.

The Kahiltna Glacier was blocked down-canyon now, and the wind was moving the cloud layers more to the west.

"Can we fly through that?" Hunter yelled.

Sam shook his head. "No way. I'm going to have to climb some and drop into the Ruth Glacier. How's your friend?"

Hunter turned and checked with Morris.

"He's better. Go ahead and climb."

Sam nodded, his jaw set, and began to circle over the wide glacier, setting the elevators for a steep climb rate. The plane, buffeted by winds, responded and crawled higher and higher up the canyon away from the grasp of the ice.

Sam turned the plane's nose to a point behind a lesser peak, and watched as the jagged rocks passed beneath the skis. In minutes the plane found another glacier, wider and dirtier than the Kahiltna, and began following it down-canyon to a point where Sam hoped the clouds were more benevolent.

"Can we climb over them altogether?"

Sam shook his head and pointed up. Hunter looked up and saw that the upper level of clouds was lowering, meeting the lower layer, making a gauzy funnel where the airplane would be forced to fly.

Sam was sweating in spite of the cold. Eenie, meenie, miny...oh, God. Now, there are two ways to fly this. You can fly into the mass of clouds and find clear air on the other side, or you can fly into the cloudbank and find a mountain. Maybe there would be a millisecond of recognition before the aircraft was smashed to Tinkertoys against the rocks. Sam always wondered.

But there was another alternative, of course. He could keep circling until the clouds closed around the airplane, or until they ran out of gas, whichever came first.

Far down the glacier, he knew, were two things. The first was a broad expanse of clear sky. The second was the Tokosha Mountains, rising 7,000 feet into the clouds. Eenie, meenie, miny...

Hunter pointed.

"What's that?"

Sam looked as he circled. Then he saw it, a tiny green speck, moving toward them against the background of the canyon walls.

Sam smiled. "Another plane, Hunter. Same condition we're in, I guess."

But there was something about the way the plane flew that suggested confidence to Sam. The plane came ahead straight toward them, then banked and flew across in front of them, giving a purposeful wag of wings as it crossed their path. It was close enough to make out the numbers on the fuselage. Sam wasn't familiar with the aircraft, but there was something about the way it flew that suddenly gave him hope. Turning down-canyon from them, the green plane gave another steady wag of wings, increased its speed and flew straight toward the cloudbank.

"He wants us to follow him," Sam said.

"Is that a good idea?"

"You have a better one?"

Hunter shook his head. Sam increased the plane's speed and closed the distance between the two aircraft. With one final wag of wings, the green plane plunged into the cloudbank, wraithlike tendrils enfolding it as it went.

Sam followed, catching glimpses of the steady little craft ahead of him from time to time. He didn't blink as he flew, until his eyes reddened with burning dryness. Then the green plane disappeared, and Sam began to search through the thickness of the cloud layer, looking, searching for his fellow pilot.

Then they burst into sunlight, and saw before them the valley stretching away to Cook Inlet. Sam let out a long breath, wiped his eyes, and dropped the plane into a long glide toward the village. He throttled back to save fuel, and then began searching the skies for the other plane.

"See the other guy?" he asked Hunter.

"Not yet, he could be above us."

"Yeah. At least he didn't hit any of those mountains."

"You know, Sam, I'd like to buy that guy a beer."

Sam grinned, taut and sweaty.

"You'd have to wait in line for that honor."

The fuel gauge showed empty when the 185 turned on final over the village. Sam pulled the flaps, and set the plane gently on the snow. The ambulance was waiting at the far end of the airstrip along with half the village's population.

Eager hands pulled Morris from the plane and helped him into the ambulance. Hunter ran back to the plane to thank Sam, but was silent when he saw Sam Davis hunched over the wheel, his head buried in his folded arms. Hunter gave a silent half-wave and ran back to the ambulance for the ride into town.

chapter 25

SHERRY FINISHED the dishes, and stepped into the moonlight to dump the dishwater.

The cabin was different, and so was she. There was no longer a worried look on her face. The time alone in the cabin had brought a serenity to her features that had not been there in years. The mountains suited her, as they suited few people.

The evenings she no longer spent poring over the trapping manuals. The different sets were now becoming second nature to her, as evidenced by a growing number of pelts in Pete Kelly's old tree cache.

She had adjusted to the short daylight and the long darkness, no longer fearing to walk the woods in the coal blackness of the winter night. Her little trap line had expanded to the upper beaver ponds and along the far ridge that separated her lake from the Susitna River.

The cabin looked happier, as only a cabin can look happy. For the first time since it was built, it was clean. But it was more than that. It had happy curtains, a clean and cheery heater freshly coated with stove black, bookshelves built from split birch chunks, and the clean chimneys on the kerosene lamps spread warmth and light over the small living area.

She and the pup had become fast friends, and several times she had taken him along on a tour of the trap line, finishing the last lap with him lying exhausted in her pack.

There are those people who belong in mountains. Those who find excitement in the perk-perk of the spruce grouse, the low grunting of the rutting moose, and the eerie opera bass bawl of the wolf on the hunt. For them, there is no longer the contentment city noises bring others. They may someday have to exist in cities, but they can never really live there. Their hearts are with the wolves and the moose and the spruce hens. This realization comes slowly, and usually by the sudden awareness early one morning that there is something in the mountains that the person needs. Like warmth, oxygen, shelter, food and love, it becomes a basic necessity.

It was that way now with Sherry. It was only at night that the loneliness set in. It came during that time after the dishes were done, and the creatures had all gone to their beds in the forest, during that time when only the lynx and the snowy owl were active.

Sherry sat at the table and picked up a magazine. She looked at the words, but thought of other things. Of airplanes, of early-morning coffee, of a warm family dinner in Kahiltna. The puppy came over from the stove and began chewing her moccasins, and for once she didn't scold him.

Checking the clock, Sherry turned on the radio.

"It's time now for Bush Pipeline," the announcer said, "a program of important information and communication to bush residents. Now here are our Bush Pipeline messages for this evening."

Sherry listened as the real-life dramas unfolded, one after the other. Messages traveled through thousands of miles of Bush to those who were lonely or sick or happy. Birthday messages. Death messages. Reports of a wedding for those unable to attend. The plight of a little girl in one village who needed a ride to another village.

Then it came.

"Our next message goes out to Sherry and the pup at Lynx Lake. 'Hope you haven't caught all the fish in the lake by now. Will be up to see you soon.' That's from Sam."

Sherry turned off the radio, picked up the pup and gently rubbed his ears. She was smiling.

chapter 26

FROM HIS TABLE in the South Seas Roadhouse, Sam recognized the drone of his father's airplane even before it buzzed the roadhouse with a whoosh and a roar and touched down on the airstrip.

He walked over to the loading area and waited for the ski plane to taxi up to him.

Sam helped Cruchot out of the plane, and they greeted each other warmly. When the gear was unloaded, Buck and Sam tied down the plane and walked over to the South Seas together.

Buck looked at his son and slapped him on the back. "How'd you like Kahiltna Glacier International Airport, son?"

"Scared hell out of me."

Buck laughed. "You did really well, though. Hey. Hold it just a minute."

Buck walked back to the plane, fished around inside, and returned carrying a cardboard box festooned with a red ribbon.

"Almost forgot."

"What is it, dad?"

"Little present for Hemingway. You'll see."

Hemingway was telling John Thompson and a tourist lady of the glories of older literature as the two pilots walked in.

"Now you take John Keats," Hemingway was saying. "Why, there was a man who knew how to describe things. Yessir. He once wrote a poem about a jug. It's called 'Ode to a Grecian Urn.' Really beautiful, too. You see, there's this jug, called an urn, and on the sides of it were a man and a woman, kinda searching for each other, but since they were baked on, they can't ever get to each other, you know? Yeah, so the poem goes, 'Bold lover, thou can never kiss…'"

"Not quite," said Harry Pete from down the counter.

"What?" Hemingway turned to him.

"Close, Hemingway. Very close, but no cigar. You see, the poem is called 'Ode on a Grecian Urn,' not to a Grecian urn, and the line goes 'Bold lover, never never canst thou kiss…'"

All eyes swiveled to the Indian trapper sitting at the bar.

"How did you know that?" Hemingway asked.

Harry drew himself up straight. "Red man go to ivy-covered wigwams of white man. Major in English lit."

The laughter drowned out the words Hemingway muttered as he fixed himself a drink.

"Hemingway Jones, my friend," Buck said. "I have a little something here that will cheer you up. A present for you."

Hemingway looked at the box and the ribbon, and a light came to his eyes.

"A present? For me? Who's it from?"

"Siwash."

"That old pirate! Why, why, that no good old crustacean! I ought to…I mean…after he ripped off my strawberries!"

"Aren't you going to open it?"

"OK, OK. Let me get this ribbon cut."

Hemingway opened the lid, and pulled out his strawberry bowl, empty but clean. The spoon was also clean and in the bowl was a note.

"Don't forget to read the note," Buck added.

Hemingway slowly unsealed the envelope and took out the neatly folded note. He looked at it in puzzlement.

"Burp? Burp! Why, that old bowlegged sumbitch! He eats my strawberries, and then has the nerve to send me a note that just says 'BURP'! Why…why…"

The laughter grew as Hemingway's face turned red with anger, and the louder the imprecations he spouted against Siwash Simmons, the louder the laughter grew, until finally Hemingway saw the humor in it and began to laugh and cry at the same time.

"My strawberries," he mourned, "my beautiful, lovely strawberries."

Harry Pete brought his coffee over to Buck and Sam's table, where soon they were joined by a nervous Frank Granger.

"Why the Sunday suit, Frank?" Buck asked.

Harry Pete chuckled. "Have you forgotten, Buck? This is Frank's big day."

"She's coming in tonight?"

"On the train," Frank groaned.

"Aw, Frank, she's probably a wonderful person," Buck said.

"Well, that's just it, boys. I know she is. I mean, you can really get to know someone well through the mail. It's just, well, you know how women take to Alaska. Especially in the dead of winter, and, well, boys, I just couldn't leave."

"She might surprise you, Frank."

"I hope you're right, Harry. I sure hope you're right. If you'll excuse me, I think I'll go over to the depot."

'We'll go over with you, Frank. Man needs friends at a time…"

"Thanks just the same, Buck, but I'd rather you didn't. OK?"

"Sure, Frank. Every man has to kill his own snakes."

"Thanks," Frank said, putting on his parka and leaving.

Harry smiled at Buck. "You know, from what I hear, Cousin Sam here has the makings of a good bush pilot. He got here yesterday white as a sheet, couldn't even talk …and was out of gas."

"That doesn't sound like much of a recommendation," grinned Sam.

"Does to me, Sam," Buck said. "You see, bush flying is hours and hours of monotony, occasionally sprinkled with moments of stark terror. Well, you just got yourself sprinkled a bit yesterday."

"I can damn well do without that kind of seasoning, I'll tell you. I'll tell you something straight out. If it weren't for that green plane up there on the glacier, I'd probably be dead right now, and I'm not kidding, either."

Buck raised an eyebrow. "Green plane?"

Sam told the men what had happened.

"And you lost sight of it when you came out of the clouds?" Buck asked.

"Yeah, didn't look around much, though. I was pretty low on fuel."

Harry Pete exchanged looks with Buck Davis.

"A 180, Sam?"

"Numbers on it two-zero-zulu?"

"Yeah. Hey, that's right! You guys know him? I'd sure like to thank him."

Harry picked up his coffee and left father and son together. Buck looked embarrassed.

"What's going on, dad? How did Harry know the numbers?"

Buck looked down at his beer, then up into Sam's eyes.

"That plane's been seen before, Sam. I've never seen it, but others have. That's Frenchy Lamorine's plane."

"Lamorine? But I thought…"

"It sounds weird," he agreed, "but there it is. Frenchy was killed in that plane on the mountain eight, nine years ago. I can show you the wreckage."

"But how?"

Buck smiled sadly.

"You saw the numbers?"

"I saw the numbers."

"What can I say?"

chapter 27

RESIDENTS LOOKING out the windows at the train platform saw a lone shivering figure standing under the yard light. It was more than the cold that made Frank Granger shake, and he couldn't help it. He kept trying to assure himself that, at worst, this would be a pleasant short visit with a woman he really cared about. After all, no one, not even Candy, could make him leave Kahiltna if he didn't want to leave.

And he didn't want to leave.

As usual, the train was late. He stood there nearly fifteen minutes past the normal train time before he saw the glow of the headlight like a rising sun far down in the forest to the south. He checked his watch again, but couldn't have told anyone why.

Finally it rounded the bend along the river edge and slowed as it pulled up to a stop at the platform. Dick Merkel, in his blue uniform, opened the folding steps and stepped down. Frank walked up.

"Hi Frank. What's new?"

"You're late," Frank said nervously.

"Like I said," replied Merkel, grinning, "what's new?"

Minnie Hunter stepped off the train, walked to the baggage car, and was handed two boxes for the trading post.

"Hi, Frank," she called.

"Huh? Oh, hi, Minnie." Frank kept watching the passenger car, but no one else stepped off. Dick stepped back aboard, picked up the phone, and said, "Highball Number Six."

"Wait, Dick," Frank yelled as the train moved. "Don't you have a passenger?"

"Sure did. Minnie there. See you, Frank."

Frank stood there more stunned and confused than ever. He was still standing there when Minnie Hunter walked up.

"Help a girl with some boxes, cowboy?"

"Oh, sure, Minnie. Say, did you see a woman on the train wearing a blue coat?"

"I'm wearing a blue coat, Frank."

"No, I mean, anyone else?"

"There is no one else."

He looked at her and noticed the change in her voice.

"What do you mean, Minnie?"

"I mean I'm the woman in the blue coat, Frank. I mean I'm Candy."

"What?" Frank's voice was hushed.

"Are you disappointed?"

"What?"

"You know, this is really a marvelous conversation. I'd love to continue all night, sailor, but I'd freeze. Pick up one of these boxes and let's go home."

"Minnie, do you mean you wrote those letters?"

Her voice was very soft and gentle.

"Yes, I did, Frank. Every one."

"But they were from Minnesota…"

"My cousin lives there. She mailed them for me. Are you angry?"

"But you signed them Candy?"

"My nickname as a teenager. I hated it. But I needed a pen name and it worked OK."

"Why didn't you tell me? Were you just playing a joke on me?"

"Arriving on the train was a joke, all right, Frank Granger. I did that for those other women you used to write to. But the letters were from me, really from me."

"You meant what you said?"

"Every word."

"But Minnie, I've really fallen in love with you through those letters."

"Are you sorry it's me?"

"Oh no, no. I'm glad, so very glad!"

"Then kiss me before I freeze."

The old friends embraced under the yard light and held each other tenderly for long moments.

"If you'll take that other box, Frank? I said, if you'll take that other box, we can go home."

"To your house?"

"You don't expect me to live in that room over the jukebox, do you?"

"But what will the people say? I mean, your kids and grandkids, and…?"

Minnie Hunter smiled up at the tall man who still stood with his arms around her.

"They'll think Frank Granger is finally showing some good sense in his old age."

"By golly, I do believe you're right, honey. Can I call you honey?"

Minnie grinned.

"Sounds wonderful. You know, Frank, I began writing you as just a personal gag. I wanted to test you, I guess, to see what you were made of. And somewhere along the way I came to love you. I was going to keep writing to you until spring, but I didn't want to wait that long to tell you. I love you."

Frank picked up the box and offered her his free arm.

"Let's go home, dear."

chapter 28

THE TWO PILOTS, father and son, sat quietly drinking beer. They didn't notice John Thompson leave the South Seas, but were lost in their own thoughts. They both knew, instinctively, that this was a momentous day, a day other events would be judged against, a day of legends.

Sam smiled and shook his head.

"Borrow a plane tomorrow, dad?"

"What you got in mind?"

"Ice fishing."

Buck grinned. "Heard there's good fishing at Lynx Lake."

Sam smiled. "So I'm told."

"Sam, I thought you had to be back at work pretty soon."

"Yeah, well, I was thinking. I mean, if you didn't mind, and if there's enough work, I'd like to do some flying for you."

"Why, flying a bush plane isn't like flying a jet, son. You have to be your own mechanic, for example."

"Sure, but then I'd know the job's done right."

"No pretty stewardesses, either."

"Old Siwash is looking better to me all the time."

Buck laughed. "You're hopeless."

"Then it's a deal?"

"It's a deal," Buck said, reaching across the table for the handshake.

Just then the polka music began, and John returned to the South Seas to lead the tourist lady out into the square. The loud music flooded the village, and people bundled up and came to dance or watch.

The door to Minnie Hunter's house opened, and two parka-clad figures emerged, mitten in mitten, then swirled into the melee as the crowd clapped.

Buck and Sam stood and walked to get their parkas and join the dance. They could see the dance area lighted by pickup headlights, and hear the laughter and clapping of the spectators.

Sam stopped short of the door and turned to Buck.

"Dad, I can't be a real bush pilot, you know."

"You can't? And why not?"

Sam grinned. "I don't have a harmonica."

Buck laughed and slipped his own into Sam's shirt pocket.

"Well, then, let me make it official."

And the two men smiled and clapped and occasionally danced as the evening wore on.

Upstairs in his room in the South Seas, Hemingway Jones crumpled yet another piece of paper and tossed it onto the floor. He stood and looked down at the scene on the street, letting his mind run, seeing with the soft focus of deep emotion the brightness of the headlights on the swirling patterns of the dancers; hearing the laughter and the clink of glasses downstairs; and noticing the dull night colors of the parked airplanes asleep on the strip, resting for the work to come.

He sat down at the typewriter and rolled in another piece of blank paper. With an uncustomary smile, he began typing, slowly and carefully.

This time, the stories would come.

other books by Slim Randles:

Raven's Prey

from other publishers:

Hell, I Was There! The Life Story of Elmer Keith

Dogsled: A True Tale of the North

• **Fiction from the North** •

other books from McRoy & Blackburn:

Cut Bait
C.M. Winterhouse

Raven's Prey
Slim Randles

Keep the Round Side Down
Tim Jones

Bucket
Eric Forrer

Battling Against Success
Neil Davis

Caught in the Sluice: Tales from an Alaska Gold Camp
Neil Davis

The Birthday Party
Ann Chandonnet